A Duet for Home

A Duet for Home

BY KARINA YAN GLASER

CLARION BOOKS

An Imprint of HarperCollins*Publishers*

Clarion Books is an imprint of HarperCollins Publishers.

A Duet for Home

Copyright © 2022 by Karina Yan Glaser

www.harpercollinschildrens.com

ISBN 978-0-54-487640-8 hardcover
ISBN 978-0-35-862299-4 signed edition

Typography by Celeste Knudsen

22 23 24 25 LSB 5 4 3 2 1

First Edition

*To Steve
and to
everyone
searching
for home*

I have wrapped my dreams in a silken cloth,
And laid them away in a box of gold.

—Countee Cullen

Someday we will become
something we haven't even
yet imagined.

—Yuyi Morales

SUNDAY, SEPTEMBER 30

Days at Huey House
Tyrell: 1,275; June: 1

ONE

June

CAN BAD LUCK FOLLOW A PERSON FOREVER? June Yang had always believed there was a cosmic distribution of fortune by which everyone had equal amounts of good and bad luck in their lives. But here June was, miles away from home, standing in front of a drab, used-to-be-white building with her viola strapped to her back and a black garbage bag next to her filled with everything she owned in the whole world. Her theory about luck must be wrong, because it seemed as if she had had enough bad luck for two lifetimes.

"What is this place?" asked Maybelle, her little sister.

June didn't answer. She stared up at the building. The entrance had a crooked sign nailed over the entrance that said HUEY HOUSE.

Maybelle, who was six years old, wore multiple layers of clothes on that unseasonably warm September afternoon: several pairs of underwear, leggings under her jeans, two T-shirts, three long-sleeved shirts, a sweater, her puffy jacket, a scarf, winter hat, and sneakers with two pairs of socks. If she fell over, she might roll down the street and disappear forever. June admired Maybelle's foresight, though. By wearing nearly every item of clothing she owned, she had freed up room in her garbage bag for the things she really could not live without: her books (all about dogs) and stuffed animals (also all dogs).

Maybelle really liked dogs.

"Is this like jail?" Maybelle continued, poking the bristly hairs from the bottom of her braid against her lips. "Did we do something really bad? When can we go home again?"

June put on her *everything will be just fine!* face. "Of course it's not jail!" she said. "It's an apartment building! We're going to live here! It's going to be great!" Then she reached up to grab the straps of her viola case, reassuring herself it was still there.

"It *looks* like a jail," Maybelle said dubiously.

June gave the building a good, hard stare. Even though it appeared sturdy, it seemed . . . exhausted. There were lots of concrete repair patches on the bricks, and some of the windows were outfitted with black safety bars. The door was thick metal with a skinny rectangle of a window covered by a wire cage, just like the windows at school.

It *did* look like a jail, but June wasn't going to tell Maybelle that.

She glanced at her mom, but June already knew she wouldn't have anything to say. Mom had stopped talking about six months ago, right after the accident.

"June, where are—"

Before Maybelle could finish her sentence, the metal door of the building creaked open. A man—his head shaved, two gold earrings in the upper part of his ear, and wearing a black T-shirt—emerged and stared down at them from his great height. He looked like a guy who belonged on one of those world wrestling shows her dad would never let them watch. Maybelle shrank behind her, and Mom stood there still and quiet, her face blank and unreadable. June referred to this as her marble-statue face. Once, on a school field trip, June had gone to a fancy museum and there was a whole room of carved marble heads, their unemotional faces giving nothing away.

"You guys coming in?" the man asked, jamming a thumb toward the building.

June fumbled in her jeans pocket for the piece of paper the lady at EAU, or the Emergency Assistance Unit, had given her. The marshal, who delivered the notice of eviction, had instructed them to go to the EAU when June told him they had nowhere else to go.

June had packed up all their stuff while Maybelle cried and Mom shut herself in her bedroom. After checking and double-checking directions to the EAU (June had had no idea what that was), she'd managed to pack their things into three black garbage bags. She told Maybelle that they were going to a new home but then immediately regretted it when her sister wanted to know all the details: Was it a house or an apartment? How many bedrooms did it have? Was the kitchen large?

That was last night. Other than a funeral home, the EAU was the most depressing place June had ever been. After filling out a stack of forms and spending the night in the EAU hallway, which they shared with three other families and buzzing fluorescent lights, June had been told by the lady in charge to come here. Staring at the building and hoping it wasn't their new home, June crossed her fingers and begged the universe to have mercy on them.

The universe decided to ignore her, because the man said, "The EAU sent you, right? First-timers?"

June nodded, but her stomach felt as if it were filled with rocks.

"I'm Marcus," he said. "Head of security here."

Security? Maybelle moved even closer to June while Mom maintained her marble-statue face.

Marcus pointed to June's viola case. "You can't bring that inside. It'll get confiscated in two seconds."

June wrapped her fingers around the straps so tightly she could feel her knuckles getting numb. "It's just a viola," she said, her voice coming out squeaky.

"Exactly. Instruments aren't allowed."

June tried to look strong and confident, like her dad would have wanted her to be. "There's no way I'm letting you take this away from me." After all, the viola was the only thing Dad had left her. It was equal to over two years of his tip money. Even after so many months, June could picture him as if he were still with them. Dad making delivery after delivery through congested and uneven Chinatown streets, plastic bags of General Tso's chicken and pork dumplings hanging from his handlebars. Dad riding his bike through punishing snowstorms because people didn't want to leave their house to get food. Dad putting the tip money into the plastic bag marked Viola in the freezer at the end of every shift, his version of a savings account.

Maybelle, still hiding behind her, called out, "June's the best eleven-year-old viola player in the world."

"That's not true," June said humbly, but then she wondered

if Marcus thought she was going to play awful music that drove him bananas. She added, "But I'm not, like, a beginner or anything. No one had a problem with me practicing in our old apartment. And I play classical music. Mozart and Vivaldi and Bach." She felt herself doing that nervous babble thing. "I can also play Telemann if you like him. He lived during Bach's time . . ."

Marcus's mouth stayed in a straight line, but she could tell he was softening.

After a long pause, he spoke. "I can hide it in my office. If you bring it inside and she sees you with it, she'll throw it out."

June swallowed. What kind of monster would throw away an instrument? And how could she be sure that Marcus wouldn't run off with it?

"I promise to keep it safe," he added simply.

June felt Maybelle's skinny finger stick into her back. "You're not really going to give it to him, are you?"

June never let anyone touch her instrument, ever. Maybelle had known that rule the moment June showed her the viola for the first time. But what choice did June have now? It was either trust a stranger with her viola or lose it forever.

She handed the viola case over, her skin prickling with a thousand needles of unease.

TWO
Tyrell

"*HAPPY BIRTHDAY TO YOU! HAPPY BIRTHDAY TO YOU! Happy birthday, dear* [unintelligible murmuring]*! Happy birthday to you!*"

Tyrell Chee looked at his best friend, Jeremiah Jones, and smirked. Jeremiah shrugged, then turned his attention back to the handful of middle schoolers from the Cressida School for Girls. The Cressidas never bothered to learn anyone's name before the birthday song. Tyrell and Jeremiah knew not to say anything about it, or even to laugh. One, because they were nice kids, okay? And two, because MacVillain would erupt like Mount Vesuvius in 79 CE (their history teacher, Ms. Koss, had told them all about how that volcano buried whole *cities*).

The Cressidas, who had their drivers bring them to the South Bronx from their fancy private school in Manhattan, had brought a birthday cake for the kids at Huey House who had September birthdays. The cake was in a pink box with a gold sticker that said *Amelie's Patisserie* in curly script and was set on a folding table that had one sad red streamer taped to the front. Tyrell liked ice cream cakes best, but nobody had asked him. A pile of presents wrapped in shiny paper sat stacked on the floor. Once the Cressidas were done singing, the little kids shrieked with happiness and nearly knocked each other over as they rushed for the gifts. Tyrell and Jeremiah, however, stayed cool. They had lived here for three years. They knew what to expect.

The Cressidas carried the stacks of presents to Lulu, who was sixteen and the only person there who looked as if she was in charge. They then migrated to a corner, where they whipped out their phones, as if major things had gone down in the ten minutes they had spent setting up this birthday party, which counted toward their community service credits. Tyrell glanced over at Stephanie, the employee who usually worked the front desk. She was supposed to be supervising but was on her phone instead, probably sending selfies to her boyfriend.

Tyrell stood there, trying to ignore the screams of the younger kids, but Jeremiah shoved his hands in his pockets and drifted over to help Lulu. Even though he never said anything about it, Jeremiah crushed on her so hard. Who could blame him? Lulu had swishy dark hair that was shiny and long. Tyrell had tried to touch it once to see what it felt like, but she'd caught his wrist and said, "Touch my hair and you die."

Anyway.

Lulu directed the little kids to sit on a faded rug with a picture of a bear in a hot-air balloon on it, and Tyrell watched Jeremiah distribute the gifts.

Tyrell and Jeremiah were like brothers. They had moved in within a week of each other, and it was like glue and paper from the start. Shared the same birthday (September 9), went to sixth grade at the same boring school a few blocks away from Huey House (M.S. 121), and loved oranges but hated bananas. Even though they were together all the time, no one ever mixed them up. Jeremiah was built like a football fullback, big and solid as a refrigerator; Tyrell was more like a basketball point guard, wiry and fast, and it was good he was fast, because he spent a lot of time running away from trouble. And though he had always admired Jeremiah's cornrows, Tyrell's hair was too straight for that style. Ma said he got his brown skin from her and his straight black hair from his dad.

The kids ripped open the presents, screaming with joy. Then the door to the meeting room burst open and a frazzled woman with pink hair wearing a dress printed with tiny kittens stepped into the room. She carried a giant cloth bag filled with something heavy on her shoulder. The room quieted down and everyone stared at her.

"Whoa," the little kids breathed, their eyes wide.

"Ms. Hunter!" squealed the Cressidas, instantly pocketing their phones and rushing to her.

"Sorry I'm late, people," the kitten lady said, giving a tiny wave with her hand up by her ear. She pulled a handkerchief out of her pocket and dabbed at her neck, then said, "I took a wrong turn when I got off the subway. I'm Ms. Hunter, the head librarian at Cressida. Sorry I'm late. It's not easy getting around the city when you're dragging around awesomeness!" She pointed to the bag.

Tyrell exchanged an eyebrow raise with Jeremiah.

"Are you ready?" Ms. Hunter asked.

"Yes!" shrieked the little kids, jumping up from their rug spots, abandoning their gifts, and swarming her.

"Now, I have to warn you," Ms. Hunter said, putting out a hand to prevent the kids from trampling her. "This bag is filled with extremely rare, priceless, and dangerous stuff."

Whoa, Tyrell thought. *This lady is good.*

Jameel, who was six, bit his lips. "How dangerous?" he lisped through his missing teeth.

"So dangerous," Ms. Hunter said. "If Ms. Gonzalez were here, she would kick me out immediately."

"Ooh," the little kids said, glancing at each other with big eyes.

Okay, fine. So this lady was really good. In English class, they call it *building suspense*. But just as kitten-dress lady opened the bag to reveal the *rare, priceless, and dangerous* contents, the door opened again and Ms. G appeared.

THREE

June

JUNE WATCHED AS MARCUS SLUNG HER VIOLA case over his shoulder and grabbed two of their bulkier garbage bags with one hand. When he turned, she noticed that the back of his T-shirt was emblazoned with one word in bold yellow letters: SECURITY. Heaving the last garbage bag into her arms, June followed him up a dark set of steps and through another door, which he held open for her, and entered a lobby with mismatched chairs scattered on two sides. A lady with spiky hair pushed a clipboard through an opening in the thick glass window she was sitting behind.

Marcus tapped the glass with his knuckles and held up the instrument case. The spiky-hair lady rolled her eyes but got up and disappeared from sight before appearing at a door that opened into the lobby. She grabbed the case from Marcus and the door closed behind her with a loud click. Standing on tiptoe, June pressed her forehead against the glass, but she couldn't see where the lady was storing her viola. When the lady reappeared, she was empty-handed.

"Sign in and take a seat," she said, her voice muffled by the glass barrier. Her short fingernails tapped the counter as she waited. Marcus hovered next to her like a Secret Service detail, his hands clasped in front of him and his eyes scanning the lobby as June filled in their names. Her hand hesitated for a moment over the box for *Time In*. The last two days had been a blur, and somewhere along the way June had realized her watch was missing.

"It's four forty-four p.m.," Marcus offered.

June froze.

Six months ago, June had never paid any attention to her parents' over-the-top superstitions. For her parents, everything was governed by luck. They even made sure their daughters' names had eight letters. The number eight, pronounced *baat* in Cantonese, sounds like the word *faat*, which means fortune. When her parents found out they were having a baby girl and chose the name Juniper, they added an *i* to the end of her name to make it eight letters long.

But when June started preschool, her teacher asked if she could call her June, finding Juniperi too long and strange.

June didn't mind, but Mom had flipped out later when she'd heard the teacher call her June. Four is the worst number of all.

In Chinese, the word four, *sei*, sounds like the word for death.

June had never believed in that superstition stuff, not caring that her name had four letters, but then the marshal had knocked on their door at 4:44 p.m.

Hearing Marcus say the time brought her instantly back to that awful day. But moving ahead was the only thing that had kept her family together for the past six months. So she wrote in the time and pushed the clipboard back through the slot, then led her sister and mom to a set of chairs by the door where Marcus had left their garbage bags.

Maybelle kicked her legs back and forth off the edge of the plastic chair. "Do you want to see my dog?" she asked Marcus, pulling a rumpled photo out of her pocket.

He crossed the room and leaned down to squint at it. "Cute."

"Her name is Nana. She's half beagle, one-quarter dachshund, and one-fourth whippet and Dalmatian. At least, that's what we think."

"She's not really ours," June interjected. "She lives at the animal shelter."

Marcus nodded. "Good, because Ms. MacMillan doesn't

allow dogs in here." And he said *Ms. MacMillan* the same way someone would say *Cruella de Vil.*

"Who's Ms. MacMillan?" June asked at the same time Maybelle said, "That's not very nice of her."

A door opposite them swung open, and a short lady made of sharp angles entered the room. Her hair was poufed so high it made her three inches taller. On her feet were flat shoes that ended in a scuffed point.

"The Yang family?" the lady asked briskly. She said it in a clinical way, the way nurses said it in doctors' offices. As if she had said it a thousand times before. She didn't bother waiting for their answer before saying, "I am Ms. MacMillan. Follow me."

FOUR

Tyrell

"IRIS HUNTER, ARE YOU SCARING THE CHILDREN?"

Ms. Gonzalez, or Ms. G, as Tyrell and Jeremiah called her, entered the room like she always did, as if she were the sun. Her long wavy hair fell over her shoulders, and she didn't even flinch when a kid with a seriously nasty runny nose ran up to her and hugged her around the waist.

Ms. G was definitely the classiest lady Tyrell knew. She wouldn't be caught dead wearing a dress with cats on it. She had on a slim black pantsuit and stiletto heels, and she towered over Ms. Hunter.

"*Moi?* Scaring the children?" Ms. Hunter replied, holding up the bag and looking at the kids. "Are you ready?" There were squeals in response. She reached into the bag and pulled out . . .

Books.

Worst surprise ever!

The little kids loved it, though. They even cheered. Their hands shot up and eagerly grabbed the books that Ms. Hunter was practically tossing at them like Halloween candy. Tyrell glimpsed the pictures on some of the covers.

Dragons. Typical.

Monsters. Meh.

Pigeons. Gross.

Ancient Egypt. Hey, that might be interesting.

After the boring book giveaway (Tyrell didn't bother snagging the Egypt book—it looked as if it was written for first graders), the kids cast aside the books and went back to the *real* presents. Ms. Hunter, unlike the Cressidas, who were hovering around the edges of the room poking at their phones, was right there in the fray helping Jameel wrangle a plastic robot out of its impossibly stiff plastic packaging.

"Hey, Ms. Hunter," a Cressida called. "My mom just texted. She's waiting out front. Can we leave?" She already had her jacket on, and her friends looked as if they couldn't wait to get out of there either.

Ms. Hunter looked up. "Sure, but next time let's put a

little bit more creativity into the decorations, yes?" She gestured at the limp streamer hanging from the cake table. "I put more effort into my outfit than you did on the decorations."

The girls rolled their eyes, but they smiled and waved to her as they left.

"Now, if you press that button," Ms. Hunter said to Jameel, "maybe it will make a sound." She got up to put the packaging in the trash.

Jameel pressed the button. "Nothing's happening," he said.

Ms. Hunter walked back to Jameel to try the button. Nothing.

Tyrell shook his head. The Cressidas never remembered batteries.

But Ms. G came to the rescue, as always. She ran to the front desk and returned with batteries in hand.

"I'm going to remember these next time," Ms. Hunter said as she handed Ms. G the toy. Ms. G stuck the batteries in and gave the toy back to Jameel. He pressed all the buttons. Things flashed and beeped and whirred. Then Jameel pressed all the buttons again. And again. Tyrell wished Ms. G hadn't found any batteries—that toy was *annoying!*

Jeremiah trudged over and passed him a wrapped package. Tyrell didn't bother opening it, knowing it was the same present the Cressidas had given them the year before, and the year before that. Apparently all boys over the age of nine only wanted basketballs, but who needed three? Jeremiah handed his gift to a new kid, a frazzled-looking boy about Jameel's age who had just moved in a few days ago. His face lit up after he tore off the paper. But Jeremiah was nicer than Tyrell was. Tyrell wasn't giving his basketball away, no way. He could sell it at school.

"Ms. Hunter," Ms. G said, pulling her over to where Tyrell and Jeremiah were standing. "Let me introduce you to some of my favorite residents."

"Sorry I only had picture books with me this time," Ms. Hunter said to them. "*Someone* forgot to tell me I should bring books for older kids with me." The way she nudged Ms. G made Tyrell think they had known each other for a long time.

"I *did* tell you," Ms. G said. "You obviously don't listen to me when I talk."

Ms. Hunter looked at Tyrell and Jeremiah. "She's lying. I never forget a book request. Tell me what kinds of books you like. Sports? Biographies? Fantasy? Contemporary fiction? Let me work my magic."

Jeremiah didn't say anything—he was quiet around people he didn't know—and Tyrell sure as heck didn't want a book, so they both just stared at her in silence.

Ms. G jumped into the conversation. "Jeremiah is my reader. He'll read anything I give him."

"Great," Ms. Hunter said. "The possibilities are endless."

"Tyrell is pickier," Ms. G told Ms. Hunter, then looked at her watch. "A new family moved in today, so I'll leave you to it while I go check on them." She disappeared out the door.

Ms. Hunter stared Tyrell down as if she were looking into his soul and seeing just how few books he had actually read in his life. Then she smiled and rubbed her hands together like she was plotting world domination. "Listen, next time I'm here I'm bringing a book you'll love. No, three books you'll love. Think I can do it?"

Tyrell didn't reply. Because honestly? He doubted he would ever see her again. Usually people came to Huey House to do a good deed and their quota of community service was complete.

Tyrell had lived at Huey House for three years, and if there was anything he had learned, it was this: sometimes adults say things they mean, and sometimes adults say things they think they should say.

FIVE

June

MS. MACMILLAN SPUN ON HER HEEL AND strode down the hall while June scrambled to grab her garbage bag before she disappeared from sight. Maybelle tried to drag her bag down the hallway, but it was too heavy. Her dog books weighed a lot. Mom didn't offer to help, but then Marcus came to the rescue (again) and took Mom's and Maybelle's bags and brought them through the hallway. June barely had time to register the neon pink color of the walls or the curious glances from the handful of people they passed before she found herself in a tiny office sitting in a folding chair across from a desk so full of papers she could barely see Ms. MacMillan on the other side. Marcus gave June a discreet thumbs-up before piling the bags by their chairs and shutting the door behind him.

"I am the director here," Ms. MacMillan said as she took a seat. There was a gallon-sized dispenser of hand sanitizer on her desk, and she squirted a healthy blob onto her hands and rubbed. The room instantly filled with the smell of rubbing alcohol. "It's my job as director to make sure you follow all the rules." She leaned down, heaved a big binder from the floor next to her, and dropped it onto her desk.

"What rules?" June asked at the same time Maybelle exclaimed, "It's so *hot* in here!" Maybelle began peeling off her layers and dropping them around her chair.

"There are *rules*," Ms. MacMillan replied in a voice that made June feel ridiculous for even thinking that there wouldn't be. "We must keep an orderly building. Room checks are every Thursday morning at ten. No drugs, alcohol, food, pets, or instruments in the room."

"I have a dog!" Maybelle piped up.

June glared at her sister, then looked at Ms. MacMillan. "No, she does not."

Ms. MacMillan squinted at them and folded her hands over the Book of Rules. "No pets of any kind," she repeated. "Rule 16.1.4."

"Okay," June promised.

Apparently Ms. MacMillan didn't find her trustworthy enough, so she turned to Mom and spoke in a loud, painfully slow voice. "No. Pets. Allowed. Do. You. Understand."

June glanced at her mom. While it was true that Mom didn't speak much English, June hated it when people treated her like she was stupid. June quickly translated what Ms. MacMillan had said into Cantonese, but as she expected, Mom didn't respond.

Ms. MacMillan unearthed a phone from beneath dozens of bulging files. A piece of paper resting on top of the stack slid off the desk and fluttered to the floor at June's feet.

"Jill?" Ms. MacMillan barked into the phone after punching four numbers with what June thought was unnecessary force. "I need a coffee. Large. And make sure it's hot."

While Ms. MacMillan was on the phone, June picked the paper up and was about to put it back on the desk, but the paper was stamped CONFIDENTIAL in large red letters, and really, who could resist reading more?

Housing Stability Plus (HSP), the first paragraph said, *will be rolled out throughout the five boroughs of New York City beginning in late October, following an official announcement by City Hall. Administrators are encouraged to move families out of the city's transitional housing facilities with expediency and into HSP-subsidized housing—*

"Give me that," Ms. MacMillan snapped, yanking the paper out of June's hands.

"What's HSP-subsidized housing?" June asked.

Ms. MacMillan didn't answer; instead, she opened a

drawer, slid the piece of paper inside, and locked the drawer with a tiny key dangling from a coiled phone cord around her wrist.

June was about to ask her more questions when the office door opened and a frail woman tiptoed in with a cup of coffee. It was nearly as big as the super-sized Slurpees that June's best friend, Eugene, was so fond of buying at the 7-Eleven. She watched Ms. MacMillan grab it without even saying thank you.

Ms. MacMillan gulped the coffee, then took three deep breaths while pressing her free hand to her . . . sternum? Clavicle? When she was done breathing, she opened the binder and read out loud.

Curfew was nine at night, and you had to stay in until five thirty in the morning, unless you were a working adult and your job required you to be out beyond curfew. In that case, you had to clear it with HQ. June had no idea what HQ stood for, but Ms. MacMillan didn't seem to be in the mood for questions.

All families were to attend weekly meetings with Ms. Gonzalez, the family services director, for the first two months. Exceptions would be made at the discretion of HQ.

Meals were served in the cafeteria located in the basement, and food was not allowed in rooms.

Kids under ten were to be supervised at all times.

No unnecessary noise, including loud music or instruments. June did her best to look disinterested when she heard that one, checking the time on her nonexistent watch.

On and on it went, making the black hole in June's stomach feel so big it might swallow her. She glanced at her mother, but Mom's marble-statue face revealed nothing. Maybelle had made a nest in her discarded clothing about thirty rules ago and looked as if she could fall asleep at any moment. Neither June nor Maybelle had gotten much sleep the night before in the hallway of the EAU, waiting for an apartment assignment, or the night before that, when they were trying to pack their stuff, find homes for the things they couldn't bring with them, and clean the apartment so they could get their security deposit back.

What felt like a million hours later, Ms. MacMillan paused to take a sip of coffee. June grabbed the opportunity to ask the question she had been wondering about since they'd arrived.

"Ms. MacMillan?" June said. "I don't understand where we are. Our previous building never had all these rules. Is this normal? Why do we have to meet Ms. Gonzalez? Why is there a security guard here? Who is HQ? Could we move back into our old apartment? What *is* this place?"

Ms. MacMillan peered at June over her spectacles, her eyes steady. "The EAU sent you here because you have nowhere else to go." She took another sip of her coffee. "This is a homeless shelter. Welcome to Huey House."

SIX
Tyrell

TYRELL KICKED UP HIS FEET ON THE coffee table in the conference room while Lulu and Jeremiah cleaned up after the party. He ripped open the top of a Pixie Stix (flavor: green) and tipped it into his mouth without letting his lips touch the paper. There was an art to Pixie Stix eating, and Tyrell was the master. If the paper got just a tiny bit wet, the sugar got stuck, and that was wasted sugar right there. And Tyrell did not waste food.

"Get your feet off the table," Lulu snapped, walking between the coffee table and the couch and knocking Tyrell's feet down. Thankfully the sugar had already drained into his mouth.

"Aw, c'mon," Tyrell said. Lulu might have looked sweet, but

she sure loved discipline. That was probably why she wanted to be a teacher.

Jeremiah swiped a paper towel over the conference table, brushing all the crumbs into his palm before dropping them into the trash can.

"Thanks for helping me clean up, Jeremiah," Lulu said, flashing a smile at him. Then she shot a disapproving look in Tyrell's direction. "Better than lazybones here."

Jeremiah flushed and started folding up the chairs and moving them into the storage closet.

"Did you hear the Alberts are moving out tomorrow?" Lulu said. She took the broom and started attacking the floor in front of Tyrell.

"Seriously? The Alberts?" Tyrell asked, lifting his legs so she could sweep under his feet. "They've been here forever."

Lulu slid the broom slightly under the couch to get every crumb. She was such an overachiever. "Housing opened up."

"Nice for them," Tyrell said with a yawn.

"Ew, close your mouth," Lulu said, leaning the broom handle against her hip. "Your tongue is all green. Didn't your mama teach you manners?"

Tyrell started laughing, and even Jeremiah cracked a smile.

"Never mind," she muttered, starting up with the broom again. Tyrell moved his legs just in time.

"Pretty soon it's gonna be us," she said.

"Ha," Tyrell replied. "We've been here three years. They can't get rid of us. We're like permanent residents now."

"That's what you think," Lulu said. "They don't want us living here forever."

Tyrell frowned. "Why not? Works for me."

Jeremiah spoke up. "I wouldn't mind moving."

Tyrell and Lulu looked at him, surprised. Jeremiah rarely spoke up around Lulu because her beauty terrified him. "What? I want a kitchen again," he mumbled.

"You're kidding, right?" Tyrell said, rolling his eyes. "Like my mom could cook anything. She'd probably burn the place down. Anyways, you and me, we've got plans. We're going to live here until we're eighteen, and then we're getting a place together."

"We could move now and get apartments next to each other," Jeremiah suggested.

Lulu pushed the broom into the closet and headed for the door. "I've got homework. See you at dinner, boys."

"See you," they echoed.

Jeremiah reached for his backpack. "Ready to start homework?"

"No," Tyrell replied. He ran his fingers over the tiny bumps of the new basketball from the Cressidas. Those girls might've given them the same present three years in a row, but at least they had taste. This was a genuine Spalding official basketball, a real NBA replica, which meant Tyrell could probably get fifteen dollars for it if he found the right buyer. On the other hand, it would be nice to own a new basketball, one where the grip wasn't worn smooth. He shook his head. Fifteen dollars was fifteen dollars more than Tyrell had in his pocket right now.

Jeremiah pulled out a worn school copy of *Roll of Thunder, Hear My Cry.* The cover, which was halfway torn off, was stamped PROPERTY OF M.S. 121 and the pages were all yellow and dog-eared. "Want to read chapter three and do our responses together?"

Tyrell looked at his watch, the one cool thing he owned. It was a gift from Marcus for his birthday earlier that month, and he hadn't taken it off since he got it.

"After dinner," Tyrell told him. "First we gotta execute our plan. You got everything?"

Jeremiah patted his pants pockets. "Yup."

They were ready to take their revenge on Maria Castro, the most annoying resident in all of Huey House.

SEVEN

June

HOMELESS SHELTER.

This was a *homeless shelter*.

The words echoed in June's mind. When Ms. MacMillan finally dismissed them, she sent for Marcus, who helped bring their stuff to their room. June wasn't surprised to find out that it was on the fourth floor.

Four.

The unluckiest number of all.

"Here we are," Marcus said when he opened the door. They stood at the doorway, surveying their new home. It was one room, about the size of their old living room, with three beds lined up in a row with the headboards against the wall. There was also a tiny bathroom with the bright fluorescent light already on. The wall was slick and shiny and looked as if it had been painted over hundreds of times, because people had taken pens (or knives? Yikes!) and scratched initials into it.

"Y'all look like you could use some food," Marcus said. "Mamo probably made her Sunday-night surprise. Meals are served in the cafeteria downstairs."

"What's the Sunday-night surprise?" Maybelle asked.

"If I told you, it wouldn't be a surprise, would it?"

"Marcus, what about my viola?" June asked.

"It's not safe yet," he said. "We'll figure it out. You should get some dinner." Then he turned and walked out the door.

June didn't say goodbye.

There were three sets of yellowed sheets and three brown flannel blankets on the bed closest to the door. Mom was already on the bed by the window—the one farthest from the door—and she had lain down on the bare mattress. June winced. Those mattresses did not look clean.

Maybelle grabbed June's hand and whispered, "I don't like it here."

June reached for Maybelle's garbage bag. "C'mon, let's set up your dogs on your bed."

Those were the words Maybelle had been dying to hear. She had been bugging June for the last fifty hours about how her doggies were suffocating in that bag and needed to be fed. Maybelle scrambled to tear open the bag, and the contents spilled out before June could warn her to open it carefully. They could have used that garbage bag when they got out of this place, which would hopefully be soon.

June smoothed the sheets on the middle bed for Maybelle—*after* checking it for bedbugs, of course—and tucked them in. While Maybelle set up her bed with stuffed animals and books, June made up the last bed, the one by the door. Her garbage bag was not filled with cute dogs like Maybelle's. Instead it had clothes, sheet music, and things June had grabbed from the bathroom, like toothpaste and their toothbrushes.

Mom, who used to cook and had even brought some cookware with her when she moved from China, hadn't replied when June had asked if she wanted to bring anything. It made June mad to think that she had used precious packing space for some of Mom's things when she didn't even care. June had taken two dumpling rollers, the set of special chopsticks they used for Chinese New Year and the Mid-Autumn Festival, six teacups and a teapot, and a wok she had really wanted to throw at her.

Mom didn't seem to care one way or the other about those kitchen items. Maybe June was just imagining that they were important. In the end, everything was just . . . stuff. June would trade everything in their home, even her precious viola, if only she could have Dad back.

Maybe it would have been easier if June were more like Maybelle, who found comfort in her stuffed animals and her dog obsession, or if she were like her mom and could just curl up in a ball and sleep all day. Trying to keep everyone together meant forcing herself to live and to remember.

A knock on the door startled June out of her thoughts. Maybelle buried herself among her stuffed animals. Back at home—their old home—Maybelle loved to answer the door. She even kept an empty milk crate at their apartment entrance so she could step on it and look through the peephole.

June got up and went to the door. There was no peephole. "Who is it?"

"It's Ms. Gonzalez. I'm the family services director," a voice said.

"Don't open it," Maybelle said, looking scared and small on her bed. "It could be a bad person."

EIGHT

Tyrell

"REMEMBER THAT TIME WE GLUED A TINY buzzer to MacVillain's desk drawer so it sounded like there was a bee in the room every time she opened it?" Tyrell said to Jeremiah as they huddled over the drinks dispenser in the cafeteria.

"Uh-huh," Jeremiah answered, using pliers to manipulate the dispenser spout.

"Thought we'd be caught for sure," Tyrell continued, keeping an eye out while carefully blocking people from seeing what Jeremiah was doing. "But not a fingerprint to be found."

Jeremiah twisted the pliers with a quick flick of his wrist.

A bespectacled gray-haired lady noticed them from across the cafeteria and headed in their direction.

"Abuela alert," Tyrell said under his breath.

Jeremiah casually slipped the pliers into one of the many pockets of his new cargo pants. His mom had gotten a full-time job at the home goods store a few months ago, and they could afford stuff now. Like new pants from a *real* store. And by *real*, Tyrell meant *not* the Salvation Army.

Abuela was close enough that Tyrell could hear her thick-soled shoes thumping the floor. And did he and Jeremiah lose their cool? They did not, because they were professionals.

"Ay, Dios," Abuela said as she approached them. "What are you boys up to now?"

"Hola, Abuela," Tyrell said, flashing her the smile that got him out of a thousand troubles. "And how are you this fine evening?" He presented her with a cup of coffee just the way she liked it: a dash of half-and-half and two sugars.

Abuela took the cup and sniffed. "Is this going to make my hair turn purple?"

Tyrell gave her his best wounded look. "We would never do that."

"Two weeks ago you made Maria Castro's hair so purple she wouldn't come out of her room for days!"

Tyrell didn't answer. It served Maria Castro right, and he did not feel one little bit sorry. She was the worst. She made an elaborate sign of the cross over her body whenever

Tyrell got within ten feet of her. Then she would whip out her rosary and mumble loudly as the beads clacked against each other. At least sneaking that hair dye into her shampoo bottle had given him three days of rest from her, since it took her that long to figure out how to return her hair to its original color.

But apparently the hair dye wasn't enough. Just a week ago, Maria Castro had told MacVillain that Tyrell was responsible for writing *Huey House Sucks* in permanent marker on the front desk. (It wasn't him.)

So now it was Revenge Part II.

"Uh-huh," Abuela said, unconvinced, as she took a sip of her coffee. "Mmm. Doesn't taste like poison." She lowered her voice. "There is a new family here today. Two girls, *good girls*. You be nice to them."

Tyrell waggled his eyebrows at Jeremiah. They loved new kids.

He flung an arm around Abuela's shoulders. "Don't worry about them, mi amor. You can count on us."

"Ay, I do not know if you are a devil or an angel," Abuela said; then she leaned in and beckoned them closer. "Listen, I heard from Alabama's mom today." Alabama was a friend who used to live at Huey House. She had moved out the week before.

"HQ and Ms. MacMillan pushed her into trying out this new voucher program," Abuela said. "I told her not to do it, but did she listen to me? Look, she sent me photos." Abuela whipped out her ancient flip phone from the big pocket of her yellow housedress and squinted at the tiny buttons. "How do I find the pictures?"

Jeremiah took the phone, and within half a second he had the photos up.

"What are we even looking at?" Tyrell asked, squinting at the postage-stamp-sized screen.

Abuela stabbed her finger into the screen. "See there? That's a broken pipe. And that? A faucet that doesn't work. And that green stuff? Mold!"

Tyrell shrugged. "Can't really see anything."

Abuela tsked. "We must be vigilant! Ms. MacMillan wants to move us into these apartments!" Her voice rose. "No-good, rotten apartments!"

Tyrell touched Abuela's arm. "Chill, Abuela. You're gonna give yourself a heart attack. Ms. G won't let that happen."

Abuela relaxed at the mention of Ms. G and patted Tyrell on the cheek. She was the only person in the world who was allowed to do that.

"You're right. Ms. G, she's the best," Abuela conceded. She took another sip of her coffee, adjusted her glasses, and left to join her group of friends and her five-year-old grandson, Miguel, who were sitting at a table by the door.

Tyrell exchanged a look with Jeremiah, then did a quick scan of their surroundings. Coast clear. Jeremiah reached into his pocket for the pliers.

They were back in business.

NINE

June

JUNE DIDN'T KNOW WHETHER TO OPEN THE door or not.

The person on the other side said she was the family services director. What did a family services director do? Sounded like someone who split up families. If the lady was smart, she would figure out in seconds that Mom was ten kinds of messed up.

"Honey, I just want to introduce myself," said Ms. Gonzalez from behind the closed door. "There's nothing to worry about."

Since this was the lady Ms. MacMillan had talked about, and June was pretty sure there was a rule about not ignoring the family services director, she cracked open the door and peered out. A tall woman with pretty hair and friendly eyes looked back at her. She smiled, dimples dotting her cheeks.

"Hi," June said. Her foot was jammed against the door to keep it from opening wider just in case Ms. Gonzalez tried to push her way in.

"Can I come in?" she asked. "I'll only be a moment."

June glanced behind her. Mom was still curled in a ball on the mattress. Maybelle shook her head in panic. She was probably remembering the last time someone had knocked on their door.

"That's not a good idea," June said.

Ms. Gonzalez didn't look surprised. "Can I talk to you out in the hall? I just wanted to introduce myself and get to know you a little bit. Would that be okay?"

June thought that was a reasonable compromise, so she stepped out into the hallway and closed the door behind her.

"It's so nice to meet you, Juniperi," Ms. Gonzalez said. "I got your case file from Ms. MacMillan. Do you have a nickname, or do you go by Juniperi?"

"You can call me June."

"Perfect. We'll have a longer meeting tomorrow with your mom and sister in my office, but I wanted to let you know that I talked to the Department of Education earlier today. A bus is going to pick you and your sister up in the morning to take you to school."

June nodded.

"The bus comes pretty early, at five thirty, but it pulls up right in front of the building."

June's mouth dropped open. "But school doesn't start until eight!"

Ms. Gonzalez nodded, a sympathetic smile on her lips. "The bus route is quite complicated, which is why it will take so long to get to Chinatown. There are several stops along the way to drop off other Huey House residents at their schools. But don't worry, we'll make sure you get a packed breakfast to eat on the bus. If the commute gets too long for you, we can talk about moving you to a school closer to here."

The lights in the hallway seemed to grow brighter and brighter. June closed her eyes.

Ms. Gonzalez put a hand on her shoulder. "June, are you okay?"

Her voice sounded really far away, and June heard her rummage through her bag. "June, open your eyes. Have some water, okay?"

June felt a cool bottle against her hand, and instinctively her fingers grasped it and she took a big swallow. She opened her eyes to find Ms. Gonzalez an inch away from her face.

"Can I give you a hug?" Ms. Gonzalez asked.

June's was not a family of huggers. Even her dad, who was so gentle he cried when watching Coke commercials, had rarely expressed love through hugging.

Surprising herself, June nodded. Ms. Gonzalez pulled her into a hug, her hair surrounding June like a curtain. She smelled like lilacs. How did she do that?

June was not a crier—no one in her family was—but she had to work really hard to swallow her tears before Ms. Gonzalez let her go.

Ms. Gonzalez reached down to an enormous purse lying next to her feet, and she pulled out a green box of Girl Scout cookies. "I'd really appreciate it if you'd take this. I have a dozen nieces who are in Girl Scouts, and I was suckered into buying way too many cookies. It would be a favor to me if you took them and shared them with Maybelle and your mom."

June took the box. After all, it was a favor. "Thank you."

"Dinner will be served in the cafeteria in a few minutes. I'll see you in my office after school tomorrow, okay?" Ms. Gonzalez picked up her bag and walked down the hall.

June pulled on the door handle to her room, but it was locked. It must have locked automatically, which made her wonder if there was a reason for that. Before she could knock, the door flew open.

"I'm hungry," Maybelle said. She held up a white toy poodle. "And so is Cleopatra. She hasn't eaten in three days!"

June looked over her sister's shoulder at Mom. She had not moved one millimeter since June had stepped out to talk to Ms. Gonzalez. After grabbing the key, she took Maybelle's hand, and they set off to find the cafeteria.

TEN

Tyrell

THE PERSON TO WATCH OUT FOR WAS Mamo, the head cook. She noticed *everything*. She noticed so much that even Tyrell had to give her respect. Mamo kept their game sharp. It was like training for when Tyrell and Jeremiah would become real New York Police Department detectives.

A rush of people at the hot-food table diverted Mamo's attention, and it was time for them to take care of business. Jeremiah reached into a side pocket of his cargo pants and pulled out a piece of plastic. It was something he had designed for this dispenser.

"*FBI Ten-Oh* starts up again tonight," Tyrell said, watching Jeremiah's nimble fingers replace the nozzle piece with the one he had made. "I saw the preview and there's a truck explosion in this one. You're game, right?"

"Uh-huh. But math homework first. And *Roll of Thunder*."

Tyrell groaned. "C'mon. We been waiting for the season premiere *all summer*."

"Gotta do the homework," Jeremiah replied, and pressed his lips together flat. That meant he wasn't budging.

Tyrell pretended not to hear him. Jeremiah had an unhealthy obsession with homework and school, and he didn't want good grades for just himself. He insisted on dragging Tyrell along with him.

Three years ago, when they were eight years old, Jeremiah had entered Huey House for the first time. Back then, his hair was a big tangled Afro around his head, his pants were too short, and his shirts were too tight. Tyrell, on the other hand, was short and skinny with straight black hair that fell into his eyes. Tyrell had eventually put on weight. There was endless food in the cafeteria; plus Ms. G made sure he took granola bars and other snacks with him after their meetings.

"You'll always have enough food here," she had told him.

Despite her words, Tyrell hid bread rolls in his pocket at mealtimes for a year. In fact, he still did it sometimes. Just in case.

Both Tyrell and Jeremiah were transferred to the closest school, M.S. 121. Some kids wanted to stay at their old schools, but not Tyrell. Staying there would have required them to get up earlier than the pigeons to sit on a nasty school bus for two hours. No way. Anyway, he liked going to a school four blocks away and being in the same class with Jeremiah, even if it meant he *had* to do his homework and study for tests.

Secret: It felt good to do well in school and not be the dummy of the class for once.

"It's ready," Jeremiah said, interrupting Tyrell's thoughts.

"Let's go," Tyrell said, throwing a glance at the growing line of people at the hot-food table. Maria Castro was sliding her tray along the metal counter, and he could hear her arguing with Mamo. Did a day go by when those two didn't fight? Tyrell knew Maria Castro would be heading toward the drinks within minutes. She was the only person who drank cranberry juice out of the drinks dispenser. He wondered why Mamo bothered offering cranberry juice at all.

Done with the job, Jeremiah slid the pliers into his pocket and they sauntered to the seats where they had left their dinners earlier. Their table was strategically located; it offered them a perfect view of the coming attraction. They settled down next to Jeremiah's mom who was holding someone else's baby, playing peekaboo and flying airplane spoonfuls of mushy orange stuff into the baby's mouth.

Tyrell's own ma was not a holding-babies kind of ma. Heck, right now she was probably in the common room watching

TV, taking up the whole couch and waiting for Tyrell to bring her a tray. It didn't bother him that she didn't appear for mealtimes. The last time she'd been in the cafeteria, Ma had complained so much about the food and the smell that Mamo had refused to serve her and there was a huge shouting match. MacVillain, who had still been at Huey House for some reason—she usually left at four o'clock sharp—stormed downstairs and cleared out the whole dining area even though most of them hadn't gotten food yet.

Tyrell didn't know why Ma complained so much. Food was food, right? He would take Mamo's food over a shriveled-up stomach anytime.

ELEVEN

June

JUNE SHOULD HAVE LET MAYBELLE CONVINCE HER
that a box of Thin Mints was enough for dinner. Instead, June
had insisted that they find the cafeteria. As they walked down
three flights of stairs, they noticed that each floor was painted
a different neon color. Their floor was neon green, the third
floor was neon yellow, the second floor was neon orange, and
the ground floor was neon pink.

They roamed around the first floor and saw nothing but
offices. June knew Ms. MacMillan had told her where the cafeteria was, but she could not remember. Finally, a guy in a
maintenance uniform who was mopping the hallway directed
them downstairs.

Once they were in the basement, it was easy to find the

cafeteria. It was where all the noise was coming from. There was a short line, and June and Maybelle got behind a mom and her two kids. A minute later, a lady with a purplish tint to her hair got in line behind them. The woman behind the counter, a heavyset lady with her hair piled into a hairnet and wearing an apron over a patterned housedress, was serving. She used an ice cream scoop to pile food onto their plates and didn't ask them what they wanted.

"When you gonna make something *other* than creamed corn and meat loaf surprise?" the lady with the purplish hair called from behind them. She leaned over the counter, pointing her pinkie at the hot food.

"You got a problem with my food," the server said, "then don't eat it."

"I'm just *sayin'* you can make something different," the purple-hair lady said. "Change don't hurt nobody."

The dinner lady muttered something under her breath, then dumped *another* pile of meat loaf onto June's plate. June was grateful that Maybelle was too distracted looking around the cafeteria to see the food. Her sister was a vegetarian and couldn't even stand the sight or mention of meat.

"That's enough, thank you," June said, trying to grab the plate out of her hands before she put more food onto it.

Dinner Lady glared at her, plunked a scoop of orange goop

on her plate, then finally let June take back control of the tray.

"Let's get something to drink," June said to Maybelle, glancing at the beverage choices. "What do you want? Water, milk, or cranberry juice?"

TWELVE
Tyrell

WHEN TYRELL AND JEREMIAH HAD GRABBED SEATS at their usual table, Lulu Vega was already there, highlighting nearly every word in her huge textbook in neon yellow. Her mom, the official Huey House hairdresser, sat next to her. Ms. Vega was training to be a hairstylist, so she gave everyone free cuts and styles. She did Tyrell's hair — buzzed on the sides and spiky up top.

Lulu looked up and rolled her eyes at Tyrell but smiled at Jeremiah. "What's up, Jeremiah?"

"I'm fine," Jeremiah said. Then he flushed and stared down at his food.

"Hi, Lulu," Tyrell said.

Lulu didn't answer. She was already back to studying.

Tyrell shrugged and dug a fork into Mamo's Sunday Surprise. Before he could take a bite, Tyrell heard Jeremiah utter a curse that neither of them could say without Lulu, Jeremiah's mom, Ms. G, and Marcus lecturing them.

"What?" Tyrell asked.

"Abort mission," Jeremiah said, jumping up and maneuvering his way around the chairs and tables like a football player weaving his way through the opposing team. Tyrell looked in the direction he was running and saw the new girls Abuela had told them about. They had fair skin, but their hair was shiny and black like his. The older one—she looked Tyrell's age—reached for a cup and the younger one pointed to the cranberry juice dispenser.

For a moment, time froze so cold it was like the Ice Age. In the background Tyrell could hear the buzz of people talking. People saying *Chill, Jeremiah, what's your deal?* as his friend bumped into chairs and elbowed people's heads in his rush for the drinks.

"Stop!" Tyrell yelled to the girls.

He was too late.

The older one pulled on the spout, releasing the most beautiful spray of deep red cranberry juice. The liquid rose in perfect arcs high into the air, then descended like a bomb on the two girls, splattering them and their white shirts with crimson

THIRTEEN

June

BY THE END OF THEIR FIRST DAY at Huey House, June was ready to grab Maybelle and run away. But there was that little problem of food. And money. And a place to live. Plus June needed to figure out how to get her viola back.

The old June was an optimistic person.

When the police had knocked on their door six months ago and told them that their dad was dead, June thought they must be wrong because Daddy was always careful on his bike and he always wore a helmet and there was no way he could have skidded on the ice at the exact moment a truck was making a turn, pulling him under the wheels.

When Mom stopped getting out of bed the morning after the funeral, the old June thought that the phase would pass and she would go back to work as a dim sum cook at the Flying Dragon Banquet Hall, where all the people in Chinatown had their wedding receptions.

Mom's boss fired her after she stopped showing up to work three weeks in a row.

When the marshal came again two days ago with an eviction notice, the old June had thought her family was being sent to a different building in a different neighborhood, temporarily. Until they could figure out the money problem.

Now they lived in a homeless shelter.

The new June wasn't optimistic. Which was why she wasn't surprised that their room at Huey House was only big enough for three twin beds with about two feet between them. It was why she wasn't surprised when she and Maybelle were sprayed with sticky red juice and humiliated in front of everyone at dinner. June had tried to clean Maybelle's beloved Cleopatra stuffed animal the best she could, but the white poodle was now permanently streaked with pink.

Sleep was impossible. June usually played lullabies on her viola for Maybelle at bedtime, but now the viola was gone and Maybelle wept into her stuffed animals for two whole hours and begged her to take her to see Nana, the dog that lived at Mott Street Animal Shelter. Was there anything more ridiculous than two homeless girls taking care of a homeless dog?

June found herself lying next to Maybelle, telling her that

everything would be okay, even though she knew that things could always get worse. And the possibility of what *worse* could mean was all June could think about while she watched Maybelle finally fall asleep.

FOURTEEN

Tyrell

TYRELL FELT BAD ABOUT THE CRANBERRY THING, he really did. He had even tried to say sorry, but the two girls had booked it out of there so fast it was as if they were Usain Bolt and Florence Griffith Joyner. Tyrell and Jeremiah tried to sweet-talk Stephanie at the front desk into telling them the girls' room number, but she either didn't know or was mad at them for changing her *Be Back in Five Minutes* sign to an *I'm Checking Facebook—I'll Be Back Never* sign.

"C'mon, it's late and we gotta do homework," Jeremiah finally said. By then, they had spent so much time at the security desk that they had missed *FBI 10-0*.

"Fine." Tyrell looked at his watch. "It's eight!" He ran

down the hall, opened the door to the stairwell, and went up the steps two at a time.

Jeremiah huffed behind him, but Tyrell wasn't going to wait. Sometimes it started early, and Tyrell didn't want to miss one thing. When he made it to the fourth floor, it was still quiet. The alcove near the end of the hallway had a window with a ledge wide enough for two people to sit on and stay hidden. He settled in.

Still nothing.

Either he was early or nothing was going to happen tonight.

Tyrell checked his watch again. 8:03 p.m. Not a good sign.

Jeremiah finally appeared in the hallway.

"Did it start?" he asked, out of breath.

Tyrell shook his head.

Jeremiah looked at his watch. "Maybe it's not happening today."

Tyrell rested his head against the wall. "Maybe not."

"If it's not going to happen," Jeremiah said, "can we go to the chapel? I don't like doing homework here. It's so uncomfortable."

When Tyrell nodded, Jeremiah turned to go back to the staircase. But just as Tyrell slung his backpack over his shoulder, he heard it.

It always started the same. The person would start with different notes and then adjust them to be higher or lower. After that, the person would do scales and then play songs. Sometimes the music sounded really beautiful, and sometimes the music maker would play the same four notes over and over again in different ways. Sometimes those four notes would make Tyrell feel anxious, and sometimes happy, and sometimes they would make him almost want to cry. It was weird how four notes could make him feel so many things.

Tyrell sat back down on the window ledge, and Jeremiah joined him with a sigh. Jeremiah wasn't a fan of music without lyrics.

Tyrell and Jeremiah had never seen the person behind the music. The sound came from the next-door brownstone's first floor, three floors below the window they sat at. Even when the brownstone window was open, the blinds were always pulled all the way down, probably because the window faced the side of Huey House. They didn't even know what instrument the person was playing. Something with strings. Maybe it was a violin?

The music maker usually played every day at eight o'clock sharp. Today while they listened, Tyrell and Jeremiah opened their backpacks and took out *Roll of Thunder, Hear My Cry*. Tyrell actually thought the book was good but the chapters were too long. After reading chapter three, they had to write a response in their writer's notebook, and Tyrell had a *lot* to say. It sure was mean of the bus driver to splash Cassie and her family with mud every day when they had to walk to school in terrible weather while all the white kids got to ride on the bus.

After they finished their responses, Jeremiah left to hang out with his mom, which he did every Sunday night. His mom would get a couple of cookies from the bodega at the end of the block and they would talk about their schedule for the coming week. They used to ask Tyrell to join, but he didn't like barging in on their mom-and-son time, even though it always pained him to say no to a cookie. After too many excuses for why he couldn't join them, Jeremiah and his mom stopped asking.

Once Jeremiah left, Tyrell could stretch his legs along the window ledge and spread out his homework. He had a little bit of math and a little bit of history. He picked up the math and worked through a page of problems. Meanwhile, the music maker played a really fast piece that got his heart pumping.

Once everything was done, Tyrell shoved his books into his backpack and leaned his head against the wall. He had ten minutes until curfew, and he spent that time thinking about what Jeremiah and Lulu had said earlier that day, about leaving Huey House and moving into an apartment. Jeremiah actually seemed excited about having a kitchen, which Tyrell did not understand.

Why would someone want a kitchen when Huey House had someone here to make meals for them every day?

MONDAY, OCTOBER 1

Days at Huey House
Tyrell: 1,276; June: 2

FIFTEEN

June

FIVE IN THE MORNING WAS THE MIDDLE of the night, not the time to wake up and get ready for school. The world was motionless at five, dark and silent and slumbering. June managed to dress a gently snoring Maybelle. It was like dressing a doll. She considered letting her sister sleep and not attempting school today at all—Maybelle looked exhausted—but then she glanced at Mom's bed and thought about being in the same room with her all day.

Nope. They were going to school.

At 5:25 a.m., June strapped her backpack to both shoulders, hung Maybelle's backpack off her right shoulder, and leaned over to pick her sister up. No way was June going to make Maybelle brush her teeth or comb her hair this morning. They had bigger problems to worry about.

A boneless, sleepy Maybelle was a very heavy Maybelle, and June almost dropped her while trying to open the door. When the fluorescent lights of the shelter hallway hit their faces, Maybelle woke up. She buried her face in June's shirt and started crying. June felt her sister's backpack slide off her shoulder and hang from the crook of her arm, adding to the weight.

"Hey, let me get that," someone said, and June felt the loss of weight as Maybelle's backpack was taken off her arm. She turned to see an older girl with glossy brown hair holding the backpack from the top loop.

"You're the new kids, right?" the girl asked as Maybelle cried on June's shoulder. "Ms. G asked me to keep an eye out for you. I'm Lulu. Lulu Vega."

June couldn't believe how pretty Lulu was. Movie pretty. Magazine pretty. She meant to respond with "Nice to meet you," but instead what came out was "Four letters in your first *and* last names. But together it's eight . . ."

Lulu raised her eyebrows.

June tried to smile in a normal way. She didn't want Lulu to think she was nuts. "I mean, hey, nice to meet you and all that." June hitched Maybelle higher on her hip. Her sister was getting too big to carry around. "I'm June. Well, it's actually Juniperi. Because, you know, eight letters."

Lulu nodded, as if counting the number of letters in a name was not completely strange.

"This is Maybelle," June added, tilting her head toward her crying sister.

There was a pause.

"Eight letters," Lulu noticed.

"Yes," June breathed. Lulu was officially her new favorite person.

Lulu reached into her pocket and pulled out a handful of wrapped candies and showed them to June. "Okay if I give them to her?" she asked.

When June nodded, Lulu tucked the candies into Maybelle's backpack pocket. "Hey, Maybelle, honey? There are some goodies in here for you later, okay?"

Maybelle turned her head to look at Lulu. "What are they?"

"Only the most amazing candies ever," Lulu said to Maybelle. "They taste like sunshine and rainbows. Maybe you can have one on the bus."

Maybelle rubbed her runny nose against June's shirt.

"Now do you want to hold my hand and walk?" Lulu asked. "I'll show you where the bus will pick you up."

Maybelle nodded, and June put her down. She stopped crying and took Lulu's hand.

"Where were you last night when I needed you?" June muttered to Lulu as she shook out her tired arms.

"Rough night? It's your first time in a shelter, right?"

"Yeah," June said. "Wait, do you work here?"

"Nope. I live here with my mom. We've been here a year, and we'll leave as soon as she finishes her hairstylist certification and gets a job. My dad took off a year ago after he cleared out our bank account. Good thing I believe in karma. Ms. G says I'm really good with kids, and she's already made a list of colleges for me to apply to next year. She thinks I should be a teacher."

They reached the lobby and signed out; then June asked the woman behind the security desk if she knew where her viola was. It was a different woman from the day before, and she stared back without blinking until June gave up waiting for an answer.

They went outside and found a dozen kids and their parents gathered in a clump on the sidewalk.

"Did you hear about the cranberry incident?"

"The new girls got soaked."

"I heard it was Jeremiah and Tyrell. Again."

"Of course it was. Who else would it be?"

"I heard they meant it for MacVillain."

"Why would MacVillain be in the cafeteria? She never goes to the basement!"

"Hey, everyone!" Lulu interrupted loudly. "I'd like to introduce you to June and Maybelle."

And just like that, the chatter stopped. Maybelle hid behind Lulu. Everyone stared at them, and June wasn't sure if it was because they were embarrassed that they'd been caught gossiping, or because she had forgotten to put on pants, or if they reacted this way with all the new kids. Birds chirped. A car went by, its headlights illuminating the street, casting long shadows on the sidewalks.

Maybelle peeked out, and her solemn eyes stared at the crowd.

"Does anyone here have a dog?" she asked.

The spell broke. Some kids shouted that they wished they could have a dog and others declared they were allergic and some parents smiled and approached to say hello and introduce themselves. Maybelle met a boy, also in first grade, who was holding a toy that made loud noises.

Lulu leaned closer to June. "Sorry about the spray down in the cafeteria yesterday. Everyone felt really bad about it."

"Does that happen a lot?"

Lulu nodded. "Yes, but I'm ninety-nine percent sure it wasn't personal. There are two boys who play pranks *all the time*. Usually Tyrell and Jeremiah target Ms. MacMillan, and sometimes this other lady that bothers them. Honestly, I think you were just in the wrong place at the wrong time."

June pulled her backpack higher on her shoulders and looked around. "We're only here for a little bit, right? We're supposed to get moved into a normal apartment in a few weeks, right?"

Lulu shrugged. "It depends. Some families have been here for years. Others come in and leave within a few days. If your mom is working, you'll probably get moved out fast."

"She's not working," June told her. "But yesterday, when we were in Ms. MacMillan's office, I saw a piece of paper about a new housing program with vouchers. It said something about wanting to get people moved right away."

Lulu's face clouded over. "You saw it written down? On a piece of paper? What else did it say?"

"Ms. MacMillan grabbed it out of my hands before I could read any more. But it said the program was starting in late October."

Lulu ran a hand through her hair. "Oh crap. Excuse my language. Ms. G doesn't like it when I talk like that. There are rumors about that program, but we were hoping it wasn't really happening. You saw the actual flyer?"

"What's so bad about the program? Don't people *want* to move out of here?"

"Sure, but people want to move into *good* housing, when they have a job and can pay for it. Otherwise they'll get evicted again and end up back in the shelter. Word is that the government wants to move homeless families into any type of housing, even if it's far away from public transportation or good jobs. I've heard that some of these places don't even have running water. If the rumors are true, we're in trouble."

"But what's the alternative? Staying here?"

"Believe me, this is better than most places. As long as Ms. G is here, she'll take care of us."

A rumble of gears and clangs echoed down the street. It sounded as if a tank was approaching. Maybelle ran back to June, her hands over her ears.

Lulu knelt down so she could yell into Maybelle's ear. "That's the bus!"

To June's surprise, the sound was coming from a small yellow school bus with HAPPY DAYS TRANSPORTATION stenciled on the side. It sputtered to a stop in front of the kids.

"I call front!" said Jameel, the boy Maybelle had befriended. He was missing so many teeth that he whistled when he spoke.

"No fair! I'm older!" yelped another kid who looked Maybelle's age.

"Hey, pipsqueaks!" boomed a deep voice from inside the bus. June felt Maybelle's arms wrap around her. "Get in here or I'll blow your backpacks to smithereens!" The bus driver was a large guy with a grizzly beard. He wore an enormous plaid fleece jacket.

"Who is he?" breathed Maybelle, her eyes wide.

"That's Charlie. He's pretty cool."

The kids piled in, each giving Charlie high fives, until only June, Maybelle, and Lulu remained on the sidewalk.

"You kids getting on this rusted piece of junk or what? I'm getting old waiting for you! See the gray hairs in my beard?"

"You getting on?" June asked Lulu as she ushered Maybelle onto the bus.

"Nope. I take the subway to school. But I wanted to make sure you two made it okay. Oh, I almost forgot." Lulu pulled two cards from her pocket. "Ms. G asked me to give these to you. You can use these for lunch so you don't have to pay. All the shelter kids get one. I think that's it. Let me know if you need anything."

June paused. "Actually, can you check about my viola? Marcus said he would hide it from Ms. MacMillan for me, but I haven't seen him since yesterday. It's just . . . the viola is really important to me."

Lulu nodded. "Sure, I'll check. That's cool you play an instrument. But I wouldn't worry if I were you. If Marcus said he'd take care of it, he will."

With the bagged breakfast that Lulu handed them, they took seats in the back of the bus. June looked through the grimy window and watched Lulu disappear back into the shelter.

The bus rolled down the street, and all at once exhaustion descended. As the sun rose, rays touched the awakening city and the rattling school bus. June leaned against the window and fell asleep.

SIXTEEN

Tyrell

TYRELL KICKED AN ACORN BACK AND FORTH with Jeremiah as they walked home after school. The sky was overcast, and heavy clouds were waiting for the right moment to burst open. Jeremiah's usual slow gait had a sense of urgency. Tyrell knew his friend wanted to get back to the shelter before it started pouring—he hated getting wet.

"Ms. Gruber kept asking me questions on chapter three," Tyrell told him. His backpack hung from the crooks of his elbows and hit the back of his knees with each step.

"You knew everything, right?" Jeremiah asked.

"Yeah, but it's like she didn't *believe* I read it," Tyrell said, kicking the acorn so hard it got wedged under a bag of trash on the sidewalk. "She asked everyone else one question. But me, she asked twenty. And her eyes were squinty the whole time."

Jeremiah shook his head. "Not cool."

"It was like Ms. Gruber already decided that I'm a terrible student. But I showed her. When she asked me how Cassie felt when they tricked the mean bus driver and managed to get his bus stuck in a ditch, I could quote exactly what Cassie said. *'Oh, how sweet was well-maneuvered revenge!'* Boy, was Ms. Gruber surprised! She shut up after I said that!"

"Serves her right," Jeremiah said, nodding.

Tyrell stuffed his hands into his pockets and tried not to stare at Jeremiah's coat. Jeremiah's mom had given him a black puffy coat for his birthday last month. It wasn't cold enough to wear yet, but Jeremiah didn't care. It was his first new coat, given to him with the tags on and everything. Heck, Tyrell would wear that thing in the summer if Ma gave him such a nice coat. Although Ma had had no presents for him, other people hadn't forgotten about his birthday. Marcus had given each of them a watch, Ms. G had treated them to a lasagna dinner, and Jeremiah had given him a framed photo of the two of them laughing in front of Huey House. Ms. G had snapped that photo on the first day of school. It was Tyrell's first framed photo, and he kept it under his pillow since the dresser was covered with Ma's clothes.

"I still feel bad about the cranberry thing last night," Tyrell said, tearing his eyes away from Jeremiah's coat. "We need to apologize."

"Yeah," Jeremiah agreed, then passed Tyrell a handful of green jelly beans.

A few months ago, the shelter had received a donation of eight boxes of lime jelly beans. Huey House got stuff like this a lot—random donations out of the blue. Mamo had put out dishes of jelly beans during mealtimes, and people could not get enough of them. They would fill their pockets, and if you got to the cafeteria late there wouldn't be any left. Folks got mad at the people who were hoarding them, and Ms. Mac-Millan ended up confiscating the bags and locking them up in her closet. The lock was insultingly easy to pick, so Tyrell and Jeremiah had "relocated" the candy to their own hiding place and used it to bribe the security and maintenance staff when they needed a favor.

"We need a plan to show them we're really sorry," Tyrell said, tossing jelly beans into his mouth.

He thought about what they should do until they reached the shelter. By that time, fat raindrops were pelting their heads. Marcus stood outside under the awning and greeted them with fist bumps.

"Get inside before you get soaked," he said, ushering them through the door.

Tyrell shook his head and droplets of water flew every-where. Marcus reached over to pull him into a headlock, but Tyrell was too fast.

"Watch the hair, man," Tyrell said, glaring at him as he slid his fingers through his wet hair.

"We could just shave your head and be done with it," Marcus suggested, forming scissors with his fingers.

Tyrell flicked his arm away, but Marcus continued to follow him like a vengeful hair-buzzing zombie. Jeremiah burst out laughing.

Marcus looked at Jeremiah, then pumped his arms in the air in victory. "I made him laugh! Hey, Stephanie!" he yelled at the woman staffing the front desk. "Did you see that?"

Stephanie batted her eyes at Marcus and tossed her bleached-blond hair. Tyrell could see the brown roots. "You're so funny, Marcus," she said.

Jeremiah rolled his eyes, and Tyrell pretended to gag. Stephanie had been dropping crush hints around Marcus for months, but Marcus had never asked her out. When Marcus didn't say anything else, Stephanie sighed and slid the sign-in clipboard under the bulletproof glass.

"Sign in, boys." Stephanie was all business now. "And use your *correct* names this time."

After Tyrell wrote *Chadwick Boseman* in honor of his

favorite actor, he draped an arm over Jeremiah's shoulders. "Ready to read more *Roll of Thunder*? I want to see if the Logan kids get caught."

Jeremiah shook his head. "Mom and I have a meeting with Ms. G."

"On a Monday?" Tyrell asked, surprised. For the last three years, Jeremiah had had his Ms. G meetings on Thursdays. Tyrell's were always on Wednesdays, although Ma rarely showed up. "Did you change your meeting days?"

Jeremiah shrugged. "She wants to talk to us about something."

"Did your mom lose her job?" Tyrell asked. "Ms. G always wants to talk to my ma when she gets fired."

Jeremiah shook his head, then started down the hall to Ms. G's office. "I'll see you at dinner, okay?"

Jeremiah disappeared around the corner, leaving Tyrell standing alone in the middle of the hall. Not wanting to go upstairs to his room, he wandered around until he saw Maria Castro step out of MacVillain's office. If Jeremiah had been around, they would have played some trick on her. But it wasn't fun to play tricks alone, so Tyrell ducked into the stairwell and went up the stairs.

SEVENTEEN

June

AS THEY BUMPED ALONG TO SCHOOL, JUNE wondered what she would say to her friends when they saw her get off of the school bus. Thankfully, there was no need to worry, because the bus was late.

Really late.

There was Monday-morning traffic, plus an accident on the Queensboro Bridge, plus they had to go through the Bronx, Queens, *and* Brooklyn before ending up in Manhattan, where Chinatown was. June and Maybelle were the last kids on the bus.

They were thirty-four minutes late, and they had left Huey House at five thirty in the morning.

"You've never needed a late pass before," Mr. Chung, the

principal's assistant, said when they showed up at the school office.

"Oh," June said. She glanced at Maybelle, who was talking to her PE teacher, then looked back at Mr. Chung. "Our alarm didn't go off."

"Happens to me all the time," Mr. Chung said.

♪

The school day went by as normal, as if June's life hadn't been turned upside down and inside out. June looked around at her classmates and saw things she had never noticed: the new sneakers Jessica had on, the way Chunhua's white button-down was perfectly ironed. At lunch, June noticed that her best friend, Eugene, brought a container filled with home-made dumplings along with an almond cookie wrapped in waxed paper.

June didn't want to explain why she had to buy lunch that day—she usually brought lunch since the school food was so disgusting—so she told her friends she had to meet with Ms. Lee, her homeroom teacher, for a project. Instead of heading to the classroom, she detoured to the library, where she read *A Long Walk to Water* for the third time.

On her way back to class, she walked past Henrietta, who was a year ahead of her. Henrietta was the best violinist in the whole school. June had performed at a few of the same recitals as Henrietta the past year, and she was in awe of Henrietta's virtuosity. It was one of the reasons June wanted to audition for the school orchestra—because Henrietta played in it. Now, though, with no lessons since her dad had died, June wasn't sure she was good enough to get in.

At the end of the school day, June was dreading the long ride back to the Bronx. She picked up Maybelle from the elementary school wing, and they waited in the bathroom for a few minutes before heading out of the school. After June checked that her friends had left, she and her sister boarded the bus.

"I was just about to leave," Charlie said as he closed the door. "Tomorrow be sure to come here right away. I've got lots of pickups to make, and if you're late it throws off the whole schedule."

June nodded, and she and Maybelle sat in the same sticky seat from the morning.

"How was school?" June asked her sister.

"Can we visit Nana today?" Maybelle asked, her usual sunny voice replaced by a sullen one.

"We already talked about that. We have to take this bus now, so we won't have time to visit the animal shelter after school every day."

Maybelle slumped deep into the seat and turned away. June heard sniffling, but she was too exhausted to make her sister feel better.

Closing her eyes, June leaned her head against the back of the seat and let sleep take her.

9

The feeling of Maybelle's fingers poking sharply into her side woke June up.

"This bus takes forever," Maybelle said, her good mood apparently having been restored while June was sleeping. There were eight empty candy wrappers on her lap. "We've been here for *thousands* of hours! Can I have another candy?"

"You shouldn't eat too many," June told her. "Why don't you save some for tomorrow?"

"Jameel says he eats thirty every day," Maybelle said. "He says there are boxes of these at Huey House."

"Still no."

Maybelle looked as if she was going to ask another question, but then the bus screeched to a stop in front of Huey House and everyone jerked forward. June closed her eyes to stop the nausea from welling up in her stomach.

"There's Marcus and Lulu!" Maybelle squealed.

When June opened her eyes and looked out the window, she saw Marcus standing outside the shelter door with his arms crossed over his chest. Lulu stood next to him, waving at the kids.

"Get out of here, you adorable, loudmouthed scoundrels!" Charlie yelled as the bus doors squeaked open. He gave out high fives as everyone filed off.

While Marcus greeted the younger kids, Lulu walked over to June and Maybelle.

"How was your day?" Lulu asked.

"Great," June said without enthusiasm.

"Ms. G asked me to bring you to her office," Lulu said. "She should be done with her other appointment by now. Come on, follow me."

After they signed in, Lulu led them through the double doors, turned left, and walked to the end of the neon pink corridor.

"It's the last door on the left," Lulu said, pointing down another hallway to the right. Huey House was a maze. "When you're finished, you can bring Maybelle to the after-school room until dinner. It's downstairs across from the cafeteria."

June nodded and together with Maybelle headed toward the office, their sneakers quiet against the linoleum floor. When they reached the end of the hall, June noticed that Ms. Gonzalez's door was slightly ajar, and she could hear her talking to someone.

"You'll have a week to pack up, get enrolled in the new

school, and say goodbye to your friends here," Ms. Gonzalez was saying to whoever was inside.

There was another voice, a boy. "Maybe we should stay a little longer. You know, until Tyrell can move too," he suggested.

"Oh, Jeremiah—" a woman who wasn't Ms. Gonzalez said.

"Jeremiah, this is a good thing," Ms. Gonzalez said quietly.

June stilled. Jeremiah? Wasn't he one of the boys connected to the cranberry incident? Hadn't Lulu mentioned that name that morning? She leaned closer to the door.

"I know you two are ready for this. It's the right time. Plus the apartment is perfect for you. I wish every family had this opportunity."

"You'll have your own room again," the woman who wasn't Ms. Gonzalez said. "We'll have a kitchen. I can cook!"

This was followed by a long pause.

"Okay," Jeremiah said. "But don't say anything to Tyrell yet. I'll tell him myself."

There was the sound of papers and feet shuffling, and before June could jump back and pretend not to be listening in, the door opened fully, revealing a boy she assumed was Jeremiah, Cranberry Incident Suspect #1. Tall and broad, he wore a huge black jacket even though it was at least seventy degrees inside. His eyes widened with recognition when he saw her. Before either of them could say a word, Ms. Gonzalez said, "Hi, June! Hi, Maybelle!" Then she looked over June's shoulder. "Hi, Mrs. Yang!"

June spun around to see Mom, still and silent as a statue, standing behind her.

EIGHTEEN

Tyrell

TYRELL COULD HEAR MUSIC AS HE TRUDGED upstairs. At the second floor it was a faint murmur, but by the third floor it was a full-on heavy beat. He walked down the neon yellow hallway toward apartment 37 and pounded on the door. The music was so loud that he couldn't even hear himself knocking.

He pulled off his backpack and searched inside for his key. At the very bottom, next to a few *get your parents to sign this* notes from teachers, he found it. He stuck the key into the lock, and a wall of sound slammed into him when he opened the door.

"Hey, Ma," he said, but she was lying in her bed, playing a game on her phone, and didn't respond.

Tyrell dumped his backpack on his bed and took out *Roll of Thunder*. He was actually looking forward to reading chapter four, but the music was so loud that the walls shook with the bass beats. It was impossible to concentrate.

A new song came on, and Ma threw her phone aside, jumped up, and started to dance as if she were a contestant on that stupid dance show she loved so much. Ma never missed an episode; Tyrell had seen her go into the community room and change the channel on little kids watching *Toy Story* because her show was on.

Ma did stuff like that a lot. That was probably the reason she kept getting fired. Ms. G had gotten her a job at a fast-food place that served sandwiches as long as his arm, but Ma complained about the smell of the bathrooms, the way people took forever choosing what they wanted, and the horrible forest-green uniform.

He glared at the pages in his book. Anger began to bubble up inside him. Stupid Jeremiah for not being around to let him do stupid homework in his room today. Stupid Ms. G and her stupid meetings. Stupid Ma for dancing around and singing so loud that he couldn't even read his stupid book.

Ma turned up the volume, and Tyrell felt something inside him snap. He threw the book across the room, and it hit the wall and fell to the floor.

"Ma, can't you see I'm trying to read?" Tyrell yelled, stomping to the radio and shutting it off.

Ma rolled her eyes, sauntered to the radio, and flicked it back on. "Tyrell, lighten up! Dance with me!" She spun around and shook her hair.

Tyrell wanted to pick up the radio and throw that, too, to see it burst into a thousand pieces. Instead, he took a deep breath like Ms. G always told him to do when he got mad. Then he walked over and picked up the book, smoothing the pages. Ms. Gruber would definitely get on his case about it.

"Oh Tyrell, you used to be fun," his mom said, turning up the volume even more and changing her dancing when the steady beat of a new song came on.

Tyrell ignored her and yanked the door open, the music spilling into the hallway. The heavy bass was making the door vibrate, and he knew what was coming. Sure enough, the familiar pounding of shoes echoed down the hallway. Scooting out of sight into a recessed wall by the stairwell, he peeked around the corner as MacVillain pounded on their door. Ma couldn't hear the knocking over the music, or maybe she was ignoring it. MacVillain pounded harder, until she was close to breaking the door down.

"Don't make me use my master key!" MacVillain shouted.

Finally, the door opened and Ma appeared in the doorway. The two women couldn't have been more different: Mac-

Villain in her stiff suit with her poufy hair, and Ma in her pajama bottoms and a short, tight T-shirt that revealed a belly ring, her hair wrapped in a purple scarf. There was the normal face-off between them, something he had seen hundreds of times since he and his mom had moved in. MacVillain with her stern posture and rule reciting and Ma not caring one bit.

Tyrell slipped around the corner, went down the three flights of stairs, and weaved his way to the back of the building. The only person he saw was Maria Castro, who seemed to be everywhere all the time. She made the sign of the cross at the sight of him, abruptly turning and heading in the other direction. Tyrell didn't stop, not even when he got to the door with a posted sign that said ALARM WILL SOUND IF OPENED.

NINETEEN

June

"I'M SO GLAD TO MEET YOU ALL," Ms. Gonzalez said. She perched on the edge of her desk.

June, Maybelle, and Mom sat on the purple couch, staring at her. June had made sure Maybelle was in the middle, a barrier between her and Mom.

On the wall next to Ms. Gonzalez's desk was a huge corkboard filled with sticky notes. The notes had food written on them: *spicy fried chicken, dark meat ONLY, empanadas from cart on Prospect Avenue, beef pho and shrimp spring rolls.*

Ms. Gonzalez turned toward Mom. "I had the pleasure of meeting June and Maybelle yesterday, right after you moved in. Can you tell me a little about your circumstances?"

"She doesn't speak much English," June interjected. "But even if she did, she wouldn't say anything. She hasn't talked in months."

June stared at Ms. Gonzalez, daring her to ask more questions.

To her surprise, Ms. Gonzalez didn't say anything. Maybelle, apparently deciding that Ms. G was her new best friend, jumped in.

"I have a dog," Maybelle announced. "She has four legs, but her tail is chopped off."

June rolled her eyes. "Maybelle does *not* have a dog."

"I do too have a dog!" Maybelle said to her sister. Then she turned to Ms. Gonzalez. "Her name is Nana and she's twenty-two pounds and she's a mix and she has a squashed-up bulldog face and long beagle ears and short dachshund legs but June says we need to change her name because *Nana* has four letters in it."

"Nana lives at the animal shelter down the street from our apartment," June clarified. "Our *old* apartment. Maybelle forced me to take her there every day after school."

"The rescue people are saving her for me until we move back," Maybelle said.

"Unless someone adopts her first," June corrected her sister.

Maybelle's face crumpled. "Nana is *my* dog! No one else

can have her! Can you take me there tomorrow? She's going to forget me. What if someone takes her before we go back home?"

"The bus comes right after school," June reminded her. "There's not enough time to visit Nana."

Ms. Gonzalez spoke up. "June is right. The bus needs to leave on time so it can pick up everyone else on the route. But maybe we can arrange a way for you to visit Nana on the weekend."

Maybelle squeaked with happiness, then pulled on June's arm. "Can we, June? Please? Can we?"

"Let's figure that out in a little bit," Ms. Gonzalez said. She showed Maybelle the big basket filled with books and stuffed animals stashed in the corner; then she sat down behind her desk and jiggled the mouse to wake up her computer. "This will be a little tedious, but it will help me understand your family a little more. Would it be okay if I asked you the questions, June? You can translate for your mom if you want, or I can arrange for a translator at our next meeting. Does she speak Cantonese or Mandarin or something else?"

"Cantonese," June said, impressed that Ms. Gonzalez knew there was a difference. "I can translate if you want, but it won't matter. She won't say anything." Then she answered Ms. Gonzalez's questions the best she could. Had she and Maybelle ever attended a different school? (They had not.) What was

Mom's workplace address and how long had she worked there? Did they have a pediatrician (yes) and a dentist (no)? When she asked about Dad, June told her how he had saved up for years for her viola and why it was so important to get it back.

Ms. Gonzalez pushed her glasses up on her nose. "Ms. MacMillan has it?"

"Marcus hid it somewhere in the security office."

Ms. G gave a big sigh of relief. "Marcus will keep it safe."

"But I need to practice every day! I already missed three days of practice when we were moving!"

"Give me one more day to figure it out," said Ms. G. "The worst thing would be if Ms. MacMillan caught you with the viola and confiscated it completely."

June blinked back tears.

"It will be okay, I promise. And—good news—I'm almost done with these forms. I saved the most important question for last." She picked up a pad of sticky notes and a pen. "What's your favorite thing to eat?"

TWENTY

Tyrell

TYRELL OPENED THE DOOR TO THE BACKYARD with no problem. The ALARM WILL SOUND sign had been drilled into the door two months ago by HQ, the nickname for headquarters. Huey House was just one of four shelters that one big company was responsible for—all the people making decisions for the shelters worked at HQ. The door leading to the courtyard, however, wasn't actually hooked up to an alarm. Tyrell stepped outside and took a deep breath.

"Hey, Tyrell," a voice rumbled from the left.

Tyrell turned and saw Marcus sitting on an upside-down paint bucket, his djembe drum resting between his knees.

"Hey," Tyrell said, walking over. He kicked at the leg of a

rusting chair next to Marcus's bucket, part of an old school desk with a little table attached to it.

"Want me to get you a drum?" Marcus asked, using his palm and flattened fingers to beat a rhythm near the center of the drum skin. It made a pleasant bass sound, much sweeter and calmer than Ma's music but not as terrific as the music Tyrell listened to at eight o'clock every night.

Tyrell shook his head again. "I'm not in the mood."

Marcus was the master of the djembe. He knew how to make it talk. Tyrell could make an okay rhythm, but the drum never talked for him.

"You sure?" Marcus asked, his body moving to the beat. "My djembe could use the company."

Tyrell shook his head again.

"Anything wrong?" Marcus asked.

Tyrell slid into the chair. There was a lot he wanted to say: How mad he was at everything. How Ma got fired from every job. How Ms. Gruber had made him look stupid in front of the whole class. How his prank had gone wrong.

"You can tell me," Marcus said, letting his drumming go quieter.

The familiar creak of the back door alerted them to someone entering the backyard. Tyrell stood up and heard MacVillain's voice before he saw her; then he felt Marcus push him between the wall of the shelter and the back of a dumpster, shoving the djembe drum behind him. It was a tight squeeze, and he had to suck in his breath to keep the dumpster from touching his clothes. He watched Marcus disappear from sight—there was no way Marcus could fit behind the dumpster—and heard him greet MacVillain.

"Oh. Hello, Marcus," MacVillain said, attempting to sound friendly but sounding more like she had indigestion. "What are you doing back here?"

Before Marcus had a chance to respond, Tyrell heard a man's voice. It wasn't a low and reassuring voice like Marcus's. It was smooth and slick. Tyrell recognized the voice as belonging to one of the guys from HQ who toured the shelter every couple of months to make sure the rules were being obeyed.

"I see the new courtyard rules are working," the voice said with a note of approval. "I don't see cigarette butts and trash anymore, although there's still a lot of old furniture. I thought you were getting rid of it."

"Marcus here has been helping us clean it out when he has time," MacVillain responded.

Tyrell heard her shoes tap toward him, and he held his breath and inched closer to the middle of the dumpster. If MacVillain caught him—with a djembe drum!—he was a goner.

"That dumpster looks full," said the slick voice. "If we're

going to get the courtyard cleaned up by next month, we're going to need another one, maybe two."

Another voice piped up. "I'll get on that right away, sir." This voice was high-pitched and overeager.

"Let me know when this is all cleaned up," the slick voice said. "I want the trailers in here by the middle of next month so we can get more families in."

The eager voice chimed in. "I'm on it, boss."

MacVillain murmured a sound of agreement. "Marcus can get it done in the next week. I'll have one of the guys help him."

The slick voice again. "MacMillan, you need to talk to your family services director. We have to get families in and out quickly. We need to move them out within ninety days for the shelter to be eligible for the cash incentive."

"Ms. Gonzalez is being . . . resistant," MacVillain said. "She thinks most families need longer than ninety days here before moving into permanent housing."

The slick voice again. "Well, we need someone who can move these families out. Get rid of her if she can't do the job."

Tyrell sucked in a breath. Fire Ms. G? She was the best thing about Huey House!

"I don't want any problems, Ms. MacMillan," the slick voice said with a note of warning. "This has to be done right."

The footsteps grew fainter; then the door creaked and

closed with a bang. Tyrell struggled to get out from behind the dumpster. A couple of beats later he heard Marcus's footsteps approach.

"You okay, buddy?" Marcus said, pulling the dumpster and grabbing the djembe drum so Tyrell could squeeze out. "Sorry about shoving you back there."

Tyrell felt his body prickle with heat, as if he were standing over a fire pit and sparks were spraying all over his body. "What the heck was that about?" he demanded.

Marcus rubbed a hand over his shaved head. "I have no idea, but I'm going to find out."

"It sounds like they're going to put families in trailers back here! And they want to make us all leave after ninety days!" Tyrell yelled. "Why would they do that? Where would we go?" He felt his pulse racing as he thought about going back to the run-down buildings where he had grown up. The buildings with no working lightbulbs, so every corridor, corner, and stairwell was a hidden nightmare.

"Tyrell, look at me," Marcus said. "I'm going to find out what's going on. Okay? Don't worry." He headed back into Huey House.

Tyrell stood alone in the quiet courtyard, looking at the weeds popping up between cracked concrete. People had been telling Tyrell not to worry all his life, and where had that gotten him?

TWENTY-ONE
June

THE MEETING DONE, MS. GONZALEZ OPENED THE door to her office. Mom left and disappeared around the corner.

"I'll walk you to the after-school room," Ms. Gonzalez said to June. "Maybelle can go there every day if she wants."

"But Maybelle always stays with me," June said.

"Why doesn't she try it today? I'll introduce you to Ms. Parveen. She's been working in the program for years. You'll love her." Ms. G turned to Maybelle. "They have a three-legged hamster."

"I thought pets weren't allowed," June said.

"Oh, Ms. MacMillan never comes into the after-school room."

"I want to meet the hamster," Maybelle responded immediately. "Do they have a three-legged dog, too?"

"No dog," Ms. Gonzalez said as she led the way through the maze of halls and two stairways down to a door decorated with kid self-portraits. After a brief introduction to Ms. Parveen, Ms. Gonzalez pointed Maybelle in the direction of the hamster cage.

"Ooh, I can see its ear!" Maybelle said.

June peered into the cage. "Cool," she said, even though all she could see was paper shavings.

"His name is Churro," said Jameel, who Maybelle had befriended that morning by the bus. "I named him after my favorite food."

"I've never had a churro," Maybelle said. "What is it?"

"It's yummy," Jameel said. "It's long and skinny and crunchy and sweet and cinnamony. Ms. G brings me one sometimes. I can share it with you next time." He looked at Ms. G. "Or you can bring one to Maybelle, too."

Ms. Gonzalez smiled. "I could do that."

June watched Maybelle run off with Jameel without saying goodbye, and Ms. Gonzalez gestured for June to follow her.

"Jameel is the sweetest kid," she said as they left the room. "I think he and Maybelle will be good friends."

"That's great," June said, feeling both a little sad at how

easily her sister left her and relief that someone other than her was responsible for Maybelle.

Ms. Gonzalez looked at her watch. "I wish I could chat more, but I've got another appointment. If you're heading to your room, you can take these stairs to the fourth floor."

June nodded and headed up, not really knowing what else to do. The fourth-floor hallway greeted her with its neon green paint. A door on the way to her room was open, and June could hear quiet salsa music. As she passed by, someone called her name.

June backtracked and peeked into the open room. Lulu was sitting on one of the beds, books open all around her.

"Come meet my mom and abuela," Lulu said, waving June inside.

June stepped into the room, feeling as if she was invading their personal space. A woman was swaying her hips to the music and wielding a hot iron on the hair of a woman seated in front of her.

Lulu winced. "Geez, Mama. Watch it with the hot iron. You're going to burn Abuela's hair off."

"Hi, June. I saw you yesterday in the cafeteria but didn't get to say hello," Abuela said, trying to keep as still as possible. She was gripping the armrests of her chair as if she were on a death-defying roller coaster.

Lulu's mom smiled, put the iron down, and danced her way over to the door. "Welcome to Huey House! Have you recovered from yesterday? Abuela told me about the cranberry juice thing. I bet it was those tricksters, Tyrell and Jeremiah. They are always up to no good."

June found herself pulled into a suffocating hug and kissed on each cheek. Then Lulu's mom pushed her into a nearby chair.

"Do you want a hairstyle?" Lulu's mom asked her. "I'm getting my stylist license—did Lulu tell you?—and I need to practice. I've never done an Asian, unless you count Tyrell, but he's only half."

"Mama," Lulu groaned, putting her hands over her face.

"What? It's true," Lulu's mom said, looking June over and running her fingers through June's hair. "You have gorgeous hair. So straight and smooth, just like Tyrell's. You don't use a hair iron, eh?"

"Lucky," grumbled Abuela. "Catalina, are you done yet?"

"Be patient," Mama crooned to Abuela.

The second Lulu's mom's hands left June's hair, June shot up out of the chair.

Lulu frowned at her mom. "See? You've scared her."

June shook her head, but Lulu was sort of right. June wasn't used to so much touching. First Ms. Gonzalez and now

Lulu's mom. It made her feel all tight inside, as if she had been shoved inside a tiny, dark closet. "I, uh, should check on Maybelle."

"Come back anytime!" Lulu's mom said. "I'm happy to do your hair, just say the word! No charge!"

TWENTY-TWO
Tyrell

TYRELL WAS ON HIS WAY UP TO the fourth-floor alcove to do some homework when he passed by Marcus's office. Ms. G was standing in the doorway, and they were talking in hushed tones. Tyrell concealed himself around the corner and listened in on their conversation.

"It doesn't make sense," Ms. G said. "How can they expect these families to move out within ninety days?"

"The media is reporting on the record number of homeless people," Marcus said. "The mayor is up for reelection, and this is bad press. If they move people out of shelters, even if it's into a run-down hotel to make room for more people who are homeless, then the number goes down."

"It's not solving the problem, though," Ms. G said. "It's

just moving families who are already struggling into a more difficult and dangerous situation."

"It's a terrible policy," Marcus agreed, "but the general public doesn't know that. They just want to see lower homeless numbers. Apparently the city is offering a monetary incentive to the shelters for every family that's moved out in ninety days."

"I heard about that. Isn't that illegal? I've already told Ms. MacMillan that I don't agree with these new policies," Ms. G said.

"Did you hear about that reporter who got into the EAU and photographed dozens of families sleeping in the hallways because there wasn't any shelter space available? HQ just said that they're moving in trailers to put into the backyard."

"For families to live in?" Ms. G said.

Then Marcus's door closed all the way, the voices inside the office now too muffled to hear. So Tyrell raced upstairs to the fourth-floor alcove, where he found Jeremiah already sitting on the windowsill doing math.

"Guess what?" he said. "I was in the backyard with Marcus and overheard MacVillain talking to an HQ guy this afternoon. He wants to put trailers in the backyard for families to live in. And there's this new policy that's going to force people out after ninety days of being here."

Jeremiah frowned. "That's a terrible idea."

"And then I overheard Marcus and Ms. G talking and they said the mayor is trying to get the number of homeless people down by moving people to hotels that no one wants to stay in. And guess what else I found out? The government will give the shelter extra money if we get out within ninety days."

Jeremiah shook his head in disgust.

Tyrell shuddered as he thought about what life might have been like if he had had to leave within ninety days of moving in. Even after three years and two job training programs, his mom couldn't hold a steady job.

Maybe he should start saving granola bars again.

"We need more information," Tyrell said.

Jeremiah nodded.

Without saying a word, they knew what they had to do. They had to get into MacVillain's office.

TWENTY-THREE
June

THE WHOLE SHELTER GAVE JUNE A WEIRD feeling. It had something to do with the architecture. If Mom had been her normal self, she would have had lots to say about it. *Ay-yah, the front door points north. Bad luck will blow into the home.* Or after looking at the way the units were arranged on each floor: *Doors face each other. The energy will not be good.*

June wandered through the halls until it was time to pick up Maybelle and take her to dinner. In the cafeteria line, she glanced at the drinks table, noting an empty space where the cranberry juice dispenser had sat the day before.

"Churro the hamster is *so* cute!" Maybelle enthused as they waited in line. "He came out from his hiding spot and Ms. Parveen let me feed him sunflower seeds. He stuffed them in his cheek and went up in the tubes to this little tower where his bedroom is. Then he put the seeds in the corner of his bedroom and fluffed up his nest to sleep in. It was *so* cute! Do you think we can get a hamster *and* a dog? Nana would love a hamster."

"Nana would love to *eat* a hamster," June remarked as she handed Maybelle a tray and grabbed one for herself. They slid the trays along the metal counter and looked at the sea of gray-tinged food.

"Hamsters are nocturnal," Maybelle informed her. "That means they sleep at— OH NO, IS THAT *MEAT?*"

Maybelle's shriek caused everyone in the cafeteria to turn their heads. She was scrubbing at her eyes as if she were trying to erase a nightmare.

"What is *wrong* with her?" barked the dinner lady.

"Excuse me," June said, abandoning their trays on the counter and dragging Maybelle into the hallway.

June knelt down and summoned the patience deep within her as if it were the Force. "Maybelle, they're going to cook meat here. You have to get used to it."

"But—animals—killed." Maybelle was crying now. "Eating—their—bodies."

June closed her eyes. Maybelle had turned vegetarian at age five, when she realized chicken nuggets came from the same animals she'd watched hatch in an incubator at the science museum. She did not like even looking at meat. Their morning walk to school back in Chinatown was filled with zigzags and street crossings in order to avoid passing directly in front of windows selling roasted ducks hanging by their feet.

June patted Maybelle's shoulders, but her sister continued to sob. Lulu's mom emerged from the cafeteria and pulled Maybelle into a hug so all-encompassing that June could barely even see her sister.

"Sweetie," Lulu's mom crooned as she rocked Maybelle back and forth. "Life is full of troubles, yes?"

June hovered awkwardly while a near stranger comforted her sister. Hugs and kisses were so foreign to her family. Even when June brought home straight As, her mom just smiled and said, "Good," and Dad had always given her a thumbs-up.

When Maybelle's sobs quieted, June spoke up.

"Maybelle, you have to eat."

Lulu's mom finally released Maybelle, then took her hand and led her back into the cafeteria. "Come with me, honey. You can sit with us, and your sister will get you some dinner."

June trailed behind as Maybelle took a seat at a table with Lulu, Lulu's mom, Abuela, and some other ladies she didn't know.

Dragging her feet back to the cafeteria line, June found herself being glared at by the dinner lady.

"Sorry about that," June said, getting a new tray. "My sister has . . . issues."

The woman grunted, her fingers fisted around an ice cream scoop.

June bit her lip. "I'll just have a plate full of vegetables and"—she scanned the options—"a bunch of those bread rolls."

The server reached her ice cream scoop toward the boiled vegetables.

"I'm really sorry," June interrupted, "but that's not the same, uh, serving utensil you used with the meat? My sister . . . well, she would know."

The woman glared at June.

June lowered her eyes. "My sister won't eat food that has touched meat."

The woman gave a loud *hrmph,* then clumped over to a rack where dozens of serving utensils were hanging from hooks. June had no idea why she used an ice cream scoop when there were plenty of suitable utensils right there. The woman returned and doled out three enormous ladlefuls of tiny diced vegetables that June assumed from the color were carrots and . . . green peas? Could you make green peas square? Then the cook smashed four bread rolls right into the vegetable pile and slid the plate over to June.

"Thank you," June said. "This looks . . . scrumptious."

She made her way to the table and took a seat next to Lulu. Maybelle was being spoiled by all the ladies she was sitting with. Her little sister was finishing a story about Nana and how June wouldn't let her visit her dog after school. Never mind that the reason Maybelle couldn't visit Nana was because of the *bus*. The ladies were clucking sympathetically and reaching into their pockets for anything they could give her to make her feel better. The area around Maybelle's plate was littered with pennies, butterscotch candy, lime-green jelly beans, and even a rock in the shape of a heart.

"It's not your fault about Nana," said Lulu. "That's a tough situation."

June gave a weak smile as she tried to swallow a spoonful of orange and green food. After dinner, she took Maybelle back up to the room.

Lying on June's bed was her viola.

TWENTY-FOUR
Tyrell

TYRELL DIDN'T SEE THE NEW GIRLS IN the cafeteria. When he asked Abuela about them, she said they had already left. Tyrell was disappointed. If he and Jeremiah hadn't been plotting the best way to get into MacVillain's office and lost track of time, they wouldn't have missed apologizing to the girls *again*.

After dinner, they headed back upstairs to the alcove to do the rest of their homework, walking down the fourth-floor hallway with its hideous neon green color, Tyrell's least favorite floor color in all of Huey House. On their way to the alcove, a door opened. It was the new girl—the older one—and she had a weird long backpack thing slung on her shoulders.

"Hey!" Tyrell said, relieved to have finally found her.

The girl spun around. "Who are you?" she asked, looking as if she was trying to hide the backpack from them.

"You don't know?" Tyrell asked. "We're famous around these parts."

She didn't respond. She just stared back at them.

"I'm Tyrell, and this is Jeremiah," he said.

"You're the guys who sprayed me and my sister with cranberry juice yesterday!"

"We didn't mean it for you," Tyrell said quickly. "We've actually been looking for you all day so we could apologize."

"We're really sorry," Jeremiah added.

The new girl paused, then looked at them with suspicion. "Who did you mean it for, then?"

"Maria Castro," Tyrell said.

"She's awful," Jeremiah added.

The girl tugged the straps of her weird backpack even tighter. "I guess I forgive you. But my sister, Maybelle, was really upset."

"We'll make it up to her," Tyrell told her. "Does she like lime jelly beans?"

"What she really wants is a dog, and not just any dog," the girl said. "She wants a specific dog at a specific animal rescue."

"Uh," Tyrell said, looking at Jeremiah. "You'll need to give us some time to think about that one."

The girl sighed. "I know. It's impossible."

Tyrell looked at the girl's straight black hair. "Hey, what's your background?"

"You mean where am I from?"

Tyrell nodded.

"My parents are Chinese," she said. "But I was born here. I'm Chinese American."

Tyrell nodded. "My dad's Chinese. Hey, what's your name, anyway? And what's in that backpack?"

"My name's Juniperi, but people call me June. And what's in my backpack is my business."

"I bet she's hiding getaway tools," Tyrell said to Jeremiah. "Did you hear about the guys who escaped from a maximum-security prison? They hid their escape tools in a guitar case."

"Cool," said Jeremiah, raising one eyebrow and looking at June with renewed interest and respect.

"I do not have tools in here!" June spluttered. "You really think someone like me"—she gestured to her high-waisted pants and Hello Kitty T-shirt—"is a criminal?"

"Tell us what's in the backpack, then," Tyrell said. "A miniature, noiseless chain saw?"

"Or money?" Jeremiah said.

"Packs of wintergreen gum?"

"Wintergreen? Gross."

"Wintergreen is the only gum that leaves your breath minty clean," Tyrell informed him. "Do you think she'll let us look inside if we bribe her with—"

"Fine!" June exclaimed. "But no, and I mean *N-O* touching. Actually, don't even breathe on it. Don't even look at it too long. You might contaminate—"

"Open it," Tyrell demanded.

June gave a huffy sigh as she swung the backpack to the floor and unzipped it. Tyrell and Jeremiah leaned forward to take a look.

"Is that a miniature guitar?" Jeremiah asked dubiously.

"It's a violin," Tyrell said reverently. "A real, live violin."

June shook her head. "It's a *viola*."

"What's a vy-oh-la?" Tyrell said. "Are you messing with us?"

"The viola is the language of the masters," June said. "Antonio Vivaldi. Georg Philipp Telemann. Johann Sebastian Bach."

"I thought they played the violin," Tyrell said. "I've never heard of a vy-oh-la."

"*Vee*-oh-la," June corrected him. "It's got one lower string, the C string, and it doesn't have the high E string. It's on the alto clef."

"I have no idea what you're talking about. Can I try it?" Tyrell reached for the *vee-oh-la*.

June snapped the case shut, almost trapping Tyrell's hand in it. "No."

"Come on," Tyrell said. He searched his pockets and pulled out a fistful of lime-green jelly beans. "Here, take these."

June looked at him as if he had lost his mind. "No."

Tyrell put the jelly beans into his mouth instead. "You don't know what you're missing."

"You all are weird," June said, but then she got a thoughtful look on her face. "You two must know this building well."

"Of course we do," Tyrell said.

"We've lived here for over three years," Jeremiah added.

"We're like permanent residents," Tyrell finished.

"Since you're so knowledgeable, maybe you can tell me the best place to practice the viola."

Jeremiah shook his head and held his hands up. "Nope. MacVillain would find out for sure."

"She hates music," Tyrell said. "We've seen her toss instruments into the dumpster."

"But she's not here *all* the time, right?" June said.

Tyrell paused. "That's true. She leaves at four o'clock on most days."

"So will you help me?"

"It depends," Tyrell said.

"Depends? On what?"

"It depends on whether you'll let me try your vee-oh-la."

"Seriously?" June said. "Remember, *you're* the one who sprayed *me* with cranberry juice!"

"True," Tyrell said. "But *I'm* the one who knows the best place you can practice."

TWENTY-FIVE

June

JUNE REALLY DIDN'T WANT TYRELL TOUCHING HER instrument, but she really needed to practice and what choice did she have?

"Fine," she told him. "But you have to swear that you'll be careful."

"Aw yeah," Tyrell said with a fist pump. Then he turned and headed to the staircase with Jeremiah on his heels.

June followed the two boys, hoping they weren't going to lead her right into Ms. MacMillan's office. Tyrell and Jeremiah made their way through the halls as if they owned the place. When they passed a man wearing a name tag that said HUMBERTO swishing a mop on the main floor, Jeremiah reached into one of his many pants pockets, pulled out a lime jelly bean, and tossed it to him. The man did a smooth swivel before catching it behind his back. Then he saluted the boys and went back to his mopping as if nothing had happened.

They passed the kitchen and headed to the end of the basement hallway in front of a padlocked door with a sign that said DANGER KEEP OUT. Jeremiah took a small black box out of yet another pocket of his pants and started fiddling with the lock.

"Should you be doing that?" June asked, looking over her shoulder.

"Trust us," Tyrell said, leaning against the wall as if he had not a care in the world.

Jeremiah inserted a metal tool into the bottom of the keyhole while prodding a pick gently into the top of the lock with his other hand. June watched as he worked the tiny tools, and moments later the lock opened.

Tyrell gave a low whistle. "That's a record," he said as he led the way into a dark room.

"How did you learn to do that?" June asked.

Jeremiah shrugged. "YouTube."

June took a step into the room and Jeremiah flicked on the light.

"Here it is!" Tyrell said with a grand gesture.

It was a large room, about four times the size of the room her family was staying in upstairs. The floor was made of thick dark wood panels instead of linoleum, and there were two rows of pews, like in a chapel. A raised platform sat at the opposite side of the room. On the wall behind the platform was a rounded piece of stained glass showing a picture of Jesus as a baby being cuddled by his mother.

"What *is* this place?" June asked.

"First, tell us how smart and awesome and handsome we are," said Tyrell, dropping into a pew and slinging his arms along the back.

"You are smart and awesome," June parroted, running her fingers over the paneled walls.

"And handsome," prompted Tyrell.

"And handsome," she repeated. June stepped up onto the platform and gazed at the stained glass.

"So this makes up for the cranberry thing, right?" Tyrell asked, casually looking at his fingernails.

June turned around. Tyrell seemed to really care about her response.

"I already told you I forgave you," June said.

"Just checking," he said.

"So what is this room, anyway?"

"It was a chapel back when this building was a hospital," Tyrell told her. "See, hundreds of years ago —"

"Sixty-three years ago," Jeremiah corrected him.

Tyrell glared at his friend. "*I'm* telling the story!"

Jeremiah looked at June and raised an eyebrow.

"Sixty-three years ago," Tyrell said pointedly, "this used to be a tuberculosis hospital. And when someone died, the family members needed a place to see the dead person without actually coming into the hospital themselves. You know, 'cause if you breathe TB air, boom. You're instantly dead."

"People don't die *immediately* upon breathing TB air," Jeremiah corrected him again.

Tyrell glared at him. *"Who's telling the story?* Anyway, they built this little chapel and that door." He pointed to the steel door opposite the door they'd entered through. "MacVillain has a thing about germs, so she had the chapel boarded up when they renovated the shelter six years ago. When Jeremiah and I found it, a raccoon lived here. One day, if you're really lucky, I'll tell you how we got him out."

TWENTY-SIX
Tyrell

"*NOW* YOU'RE GOING TO LET ME TRY your viola, right?" Tyrell asked June, looking at her instrument case.

June looked at him. "How can I be *really* sure that it's okay to practice in here?"

"MacVillain never comes down here," Tyrell confirmed. "Weren't you paying attention to my tuberculosis story? *And* she left hours ago."

June looked wary. "You know I don't let anyone touch this, right?"

"Not even your mom?"

"Nope. Not my mom, and not Maybelle." June unzipped her case.

Jeremiah took a seat near the back of the room, reached under the pew, and pulled out a box of jelly beans. He walked over to June and waited for her to put down her bow so he could pour some into her hand.

"Thanks," she said, and put a few in her mouth. "Hey, these are good."

"Don't eat them all," he told her. "They're handy when you need Huey House staff to do you favors, like ignoring the fact that you're using this space to practice."

"I can't get in here without you anyway. I don't know how to pick locks."

Jeremiah pulled a small key out of yet *another* pocket of his pants and tossed it into June's viola case.

"You have a *key?* Why do you pick the lock, then?" June asked.

Jeremiah shrugged. "For fun."

"Play something," Tyrell said to June.

"What composer do you like?" she asked, lifting the viola to her shoulder while twisting the wood things at the top and running her bow across the strings. The sound from the strings grew sweeter and cleaner. "Bach? Pachelbel? Telemann?"

"I don't know who any of those people are."

"I'll start with the first movement of the Telemann Viola

Concerto in G Major. His musical phrasing is easy to understand. Let me warm up my fingers." She played some very slow scales. When she finished, she paused and took a deep breath. Then her bow played the first note and filled the room with perfect vibrations. She only played for a couple of minutes, but when her bow lifted off the last note Tyrell let out a breath. He wished the piece were a lot longer. June paused for a few moments before bringing her viola down and looking at them expectantly.

"I haven't been able to practice like I should," June said. "It's hard when you haven't had lessons in months."

Tyrell stared at her. Was she kidding? Her playing was amazing! "How can I play like that?"

"Well," June said, "I've been playing since I was four. If you want to learn, you'll need lessons. Maybe your school has them?"

"Our school doesn't have instrument lessons," Jeremiah said. "My mom asked about it."

"Can I try your viola now?" Tyrell asked.

June hesitated. "My dad gave it to me, and it's really special . . ."

Before Tyrell could try to persuade her, his watch beeped. It was eight o'clock.

"Gotta go," he said, heading for the door.

"Where are you—" June started.

"You coming?" Tyrell asked Jeremiah.

He shook his head. "I'll stay and finish my homework here."

Tyrell shrugged, jogged out of the chapel, and dashed upstairs. He did not want to be late for the music.

TWENTY-SEVEN

June

JUNE PRACTICED FOR AN HOUR BEFORE JEREMIAH told her it was curfew and they had to get back to their rooms. He tried to convince her that it was safer to keep the viola in the chapel rather than bring it up to her room—Ms. MacMillan sometimes made surprise room checks—but June couldn't bear to be without it.

Jeremiah didn't seem to be in the mood to talk, so even though she was curious, June didn't ask him about the conversation she had overheard when he was in Ms. Gonzalez's office. He said goodbye to her as they passed the third floor, and June continued up to the fourth.

She was relieved to see that Maybelle was still asleep.

Mom was also asleep, or at least, June thought she was. It was hard to tell when she was facing the other direction.

June went into the tiny bathroom and brushed her teeth and changed into her pajamas. When she was done, she sat on Maybelle's bed, moving some of her stuffed animals off to the side to make space.

Maybelle stirred, then murmured, "Pray for Nana."

"I will," June said, tucking the blanket in all around her so she looked like a cocooned caterpillar.

"Play the lullaby by Brahms, please," Maybelle said sleepily.

"Okay."

"Don't leave," Maybelle said.

"I won't," June answered. She leaned over and opened her viola case and tightened her bow. The room was dimly lit from the streetlamps outside their window. She sat back down on Maybelle's bed, playing Brahms's familiar Lullaby as pianissimo as possible, repeating the melody over and over again until Maybelle's breathing was even.

Mom got out of bed and shuffled to the bathroom. A few minutes later, she emerged and headed right back to bed. It was as if they didn't exist.

June sat there, her viola across her lap, listening to the sounds of Maybelle's light snoring and the chatter and laughter of people in the hallway. She missed the familiar sounds of nighttime in Chinatown: the rattle of chains from storefront gates being pulled down at closing time and conversations spoken in Chinese lulling her to sleep with the rise and fall of the language's tones.

Only when the shelter grew quiet did June nestle her viola back in its case. Just how long would they be here?

TUESDAY, OCTOBER 2

Days at Huey House
Tyrell: 1,277; June: 3

TWENTY-EIGHT

Tyrell

TYRELL WALKED HOME FROM SCHOOL ALONE THE next day. He had also walked to school alone. Jeremiah had had to go to school early with his mom to meet with Ms. Gruber, and Tyrell figured it was the same old discussion, the one where Ms. Gruber would tell Jeremiah that he had so much potential but needed to speak up in class and cooperate in group projects because participation was a key piece of the grade. It didn't make much sense to Tyrell, since the teachers kept telling him to *stop* participating so much.

It was weird that teachers always wanted you to do the opposite of what you were doing.

Jeremiah had acted strange after school. "I have to run home," he had said. "Meeting with Ms. G."

"You had your meeting yesterday!" Tyrell yelled at his friend's retreating back. But Jeremiah had already turned the corner and disappeared, and there was no way Tyrell was going to chase him, not with so many books weighing down his backpack. When Ms. Walker, the school librarian, had found out that he didn't hate *Roll of Thunder, Hear My Cry*, she'd been so thrilled that she gave Tyrell *more* stuff to read: *Chains*, *New Kid*, and *When Stars Are Scattered*.

Tyrell was going to tell Ms. Walker that it would take years to read those books, way beyond the two-week checkout limit, but Ms. Walker was already pushing books into another kid's hands. So now he had to carry around three hardcover books, which made the nylon ropes of his bag cut into his shoulders. He preferred to keep his backpack light enough that he could play basketball without taking it off and risk having it stolen.

It was annoying that Jeremiah was suddenly so busy, especially with everything going on at Huey House. The night before, Tyrell hadn't been able to sleep because he'd been thinking about what that guy from HQ said about the new housing program. He was about to turn off the bustling boulevard when a man emerged from Pet Outlet, struggling with the door as he balanced a huge bag of dog food on his shoulder—larger than the fifty-pound bags of rice Mamo ordered for the cafeteria—while holding a small cardboard box punched with holes.

Tyrell reached over and grabbed the door for him. The man was wearing a Yankees shirt—#2, Jeter, so he must have been a good person.

"Thanks," he said.

"What's in the box?" Tyrell asked.

"Mice for my python," the man said.

"Whoa. You have a snake?"

"Yeah," the man said. "My wife hates it, especially at feeding time. The snake swallows the mice whole. It's awesome."

The man propped the dog food against the wall of the store so he could grab his wallet from his back pocket. "Thanks for helping me out, kid. Go treat yourself." He pushed a five-dollar bill into Tyrell's hand, balanced the dog food back on his shoulder, and walked toward the bus stop.

Five dollars! Tyrell considered running after the man and returning the money—he felt weird taking it just because he had opened a door—but he looked at the pet store again and an idea popped into his brain.

Tyrell opened the dingy door and a bell on the inside handle jingled. He stepped in. The floors were covered in peeling linoleum and the shelves were loaded with dusty bags of cat litter, pet food, and faded chew toys. In the back corner of the store by the cash register was a large glass tank lit from above, filled with small white mice scurrying over each other.

"Can I help you?" A guy wearing a grungy Pet Outlet hat leaned over the counter and looked at Tyrell.

Tyrell glanced at him, then back at the white mice, letting his fingers run over the creases of the bill in his hand. "How many of these mice can I get for five dollars?"

"Two for a buck," replied the man.

Tyrell pushed the bill across the table and the man got to work plucking mice out of the tank and putting them into a cardboard box. While he waited, a newspaper on the counter next to the register caught his attention. The headline, in big, bold white letters against a dark photo of a man sleeping on the street, read HOMELESS POPULATION SURGES.

TWENTY-NINE
June

IT HAD BEEN A LONG DAY.

Once again, she and Maybelle had woken up at five fifteen.

They were outside the shelter by five thirty.

Then the long ride to school.

June fell asleep in math class and got scolded by Mr. Torres.

She sat with her friends at lunch but told them she had forgotten her lunch at home. Eugene offered to share his, then looked concerned when she declined.

It was a long ride back to the Bronx.

They finally returned to Huey House at four thirty in the afternoon. After confirming with Stephanie that Ms. MacMillan was gone for the day, June and Maybelle went upstairs to their room so June could pick up her viola before she brought Maybelle to the after-school room. Mom didn't say anything when they arrived or when they left.

Maybelle continued to chatter on about Churro the hamster, a topic she had not strayed from the entire way home on the bus, even when June had dozed off. June had decided it was better than listening to Maybelle sigh over Nana. When they got to the basement, Maybelle rushed into the after-school room and beelined for the hamster cage.

"I got lots of books from the library to read to you," Maybelle told Churro as she unzipped her backpack. "This book is called *Jenny and the Cat Club*." She showed Churro the cover.

June watched Churro sleep while Maybelle read. A few minutes later, Tyrell joined them.

"Hey," Tyrell said, glancing at June's viola case. "Are you going to play that vee-oh-la today?"

"I'm about to practice," June told him.

Maybelle noticed Tyrell. "I'm Maybelle," she said to him. "Want me to read to you? Oh, look at Churro! I think he winked at me!"

June glanced at Churro. The hamster was still fast asleep in his nest of shavings, surrounded by nuts and seeds. One corner of his sleeping space was filled with tiny poop pellets.

"Um. Yeah. I guess," Tyrell said.

"It's nice here." Maybelle looked around. "June wishes we were back at home, but I like all the books and I like Churro and I like Ms. Gonzalez. There's lots of people to talk to. What do you like to read?" she asked him.

The high-pitched screams of other kids arriving filled June's ears, and that was her cue to get to the chapel.

"I'm going to practice," June told Maybelle and Tyrell.

"I'll come with you," Tyrell said hastily. When they were out of Maybelle's earshot, he leaned toward June and said, "Your sister talks *a lot*."

"Yep," June said as they left the after-school room. "Hey, where did you run off to last night?"

Before he could answer, they bumped into Abuela and Jeremiah.

"Hey," Jeremiah said.

"Just the girl I was looking for," Abuela said, pointing a finger at June.

"Me?" June said, pointing at herself.

"I heard you last night," she said. "You play beautifully. And you are very lucky, because I know the perfect person to be your teacher."

"I am *not* lucky," June told her. If she were lucky, she wouldn't be here. She would have had a viola lesson in the past six months. And she would have had a father who was alive and a mother who had a job and took care of her.

"Yes you are, because you will have lessons now," Abuela said, as if she had just saved the world's population of honey-bees. "All you have to do is go next door."

"I . . . don't think that's a great idea," June told her. How would she smuggle the viola in and out of the shelter? And didn't lessons cost money?

"I've already talked to Domenika and set up a lesson for you tonight," Abuela said. "If you don't like her, you don't have to keep going. But she is magic with the violin, I tell you."

"But I don't play the violin. I play the viola."

"Violin, vy-oh-la, it is fine. She plays both."

"It's *vee*-oh-la," Jeremiah corrected her.

"I don't have money for lessons," June said.

"Do not worry, I handled it."

"How about getting my viola in and out of Huey House? You know if Ms. MacMillan sees it—"

"Your lesson is at seven," Abuela interrupted. "Ms. Mac-Millan is already gone. Taking the vy-oh-la out of here will not be a problem."

June was torn. On the one hand, she needed lessons if she was to have any chance of doing well at her school's orchestra auditions. On the other hand, she had no idea who Domenika was.

"Are you saying," Tyrell said slowly, "that June is going to the place where the music comes from every night? June is taking lessons from *her?*"

"That is exactly right," Abuela said.

Tyrell looked at June. "You *are* lucky!"

THIRTY
Tyrell

JUNE WAS GOING TO TAKE LESSONS FROM the violin lady next door, and Tyrell was going to be there for it.

"You're going," he told her. "End of story."

"End of story," Abuela echoed.

"Fine," June said, looking at their determined faces. "I'll try it once. If it doesn't work, I'm not going again."

"Fine," Abuela said. "You will come to me tonight after your lesson, and you will thank me." She spun on her heel and strode down the hallway, the corridor ringing with the echoes of her footsteps.

"Hey!" Tyrell said to June. "You're officially a part of Huey House! Initiation is complete only after a lecture by Abuela."

"It's happened to all of us," Jeremiah added.

June shook her head. "She didn't give me the option of saying no. What if this 'teacher' " —June curved her fingers into quote marks— "is a psychopath? Or what if she took a year of viola in high school and thinks she's some kind of professional?"

"If she is who I think she is," Tyrell said, "then she *definitely* knows what she's doing."

"You know her?"

Tyrell and Jeremiah exchanged looks.

"We listen to her every night from the fourth floor," Tyrell said.

"*You* listen to her every night," Jeremiah corrected Tyrell. "I *sometimes* do."

"Whatever," Tyrell said. "There's a window ledge at the end of the hall where we sit. She practices every night at eight o'clock, and tonight I am going with you to meet her."

June sighed. "I'm not sure about all this."

Tyrell was about to respond when the hairs on the back of his neck tingled. He had to act fast. He reached down and swept June's viola off the ground.

"What the heck, Tyrell? Give that back!" June shrieked.

Tyrell ran down the hall with the instrument. "Trust me!"

"Tyrell!" June yelled, running after him. "Give it back!

You're such a"—Tyrell kept going, but he felt a bit of his heart ice over at what he knew was coming next—"criminal!"

He slipped into the stairwell and charged up the four flights. Dropping the instrument in front of June's door, he bent over and put his hands on his knees, lungs on fire.

THIRTY-ONE

June

JUNE HEARD THE ELEVATOR DOOR OPEN AS she chased Tyrell, and just as she was passing it, Ms. MacMillan stepped out into the hallway. June ran into her and fell to the ground.

"*What* is going *on* down here?" Ms. MacMillan screeched as she stumbled into the wall, her voice hitting an octave June's ears had never registered before. Ms. MacMillan yanked the container of hand sanitizer dangling from her purse, squirted a healthy blob on her hands, and scrubbed as if she were a surgeon prepping for the operating room.

June picked herself up.

"No running in the hallways," Ms. MacMillan said. "Is it true that there's an instrument on the property?" Her nose twitched, as if she could sniff it out, but then the after-school-room door swung open and a dozen screaming kids rushed out like a raging river. Maybelle was one of them, but she had a book open and was reading it while she walked across the hallway to the cafeteria and didn't even notice her sister. Ms. MacMillan flattened herself against the wall to avoid kids brushing against her.

"I'm sorry for running," June said, then edged toward the stairwell. She needed to find Tyrell . . . to apologize big-time. "I'll never do it again."

Ms. MacMillan peered around suspiciously; then, deeming the basement instrument-free, she used her elbow to press the elevator button. "I always regret coming down here," Ms. MacMillan muttered as the door opened and she disappeared from sight.

June found herself standing in the hallway with Jeremiah, alone. The kids had beelined for the cafeteria for a snack, and the sounds of talking and laughing poured from the dining area.

Jeremiah looked at her for a long moment, then followed the kids to the cafeteria without saying goodbye.

June raced through Huey House looking for Tyrell, but he was nowhere to be found. Finally, she headed slowly up the stairs to the fourth floor.

Her viola sat outside her door.

June went into her room and stashed the viola under her bed. Mom, surprisingly, was not in her bed. She wasn't in the bathroom, either. June briefly wondered where her mother had gone, but then, to her surprise, she realized she just didn't care that much.

Curling up into a ball, June wished she were back in their apartment. She imagined her dad coming into her bedroom to tell her a story about his shift at the restaurant and the characters he had met while doing deliveries. Once, a guy had opened his door wearing a Spider-Man costume . . . and it wasn't Halloween. Another time, a woman opened the door and Dad had counted eighteen cats roaming around while he waited for the woman to find exact change.

June must have drifted off to sleep, because the sound of a door slamming down the hall woke her. Checking her watch, she realized it was time to pick up Maybelle.

June headed to the basement and met her sister, and together they went across the hall to the cafeteria, where they got dinner without incident. Tyrell and Jeremiah were nowhere to be seen. Even though she wanted to stick around and wait for them, she had to get Maybelle upstairs before her lesson.

Up in their room, Mom had returned and was back in her

bed. It didn't take long to get Maybelle ready for sleep. Her sister kept up a steady stream of chatter about Churro and Jameel and even forgot to ask June to play her usual lullabies. Getting up at five in the morning was wearing her out. June tucked the covers under Maybelle's chin and sat on the edge of the bed, watching her sister's eyes flutter, then listened as her breathing evened. After waiting a few more minutes to make sure she was asleep, June shrugged on her jacket and grabbed her viola from under the bed.

"Néih hái bīndouh ah?" came Mom's voice from the far side of the room. *Where are you going?*

June startled at the sound. It had been so long since Mom had spoken to her. Weeks? Months? June opened the door and a strip of orange light from the hallway spilled across the room.

"Jèhjè—" Mom said, sitting up. Jèhjè was what her parents had always called her; it meant *big sister*.

June responded by shutting the door, her heart beating against the armor she had built around it. Downstairs, Marcus was manning the front desk—Stephanie must have been on break—and he gave her an easy grin as she picked up a pen to sign out.

"Curfew at nine," he reminded her.

"I know," June said, filling out the lines of the sheet. She put the pen down and looked at Marcus, who was now reading his book. His face was scruffy. Her mom had always told her that facial hair gave people bad luck, another Chinese super-stition. Marcus, however, didn't seem concerned about luck. He was tipped back in his chair, balancing on the back two legs. June herself had never sat in a chair like that. Why test luck, right?

"Hey, Marcus?"

"What's up?"

June looked away and fiddled with the straps of her viola case. "I sort of . . . messed up."

He closed his book and brought his chair legs back to the ground. "Want to talk about it?"

June hesitated. She was so used to being the one who got it right, did the right thing, made the right choices. She took care of her sister and kept the family together. She cleaned the bathroom even though she hated it, remembered people's birthdays, and tried to eat meals as recommended on the USDA food pyramid. The bitterness of being wrong was hard to swallow.

As June told Marcus about what had happened downstairs, Marcus listened with his head bowed and his hands folded on the desk. When she finished talking, he looked up.

June pinned her gaze to a point beyond his shoulder; she couldn't meet his eyes.

"We all make mistakes," Marcus said slowly. "Sometimes

we fall under the weight of other people's mistakes. Tyrell will always question himself because of his past. I suggest that you apologize to him, then give him time."

June nodded. She could understand that fear. The sound of the shelter doors opening sparked hope that it was Tyrell, ready to go to the lesson with her, but it was only Stephanie returning from break.

Marcus flashed June a smile as he stood to give Stephanie her seat. "Keep your head up."

He buzzed open the doors, and June stepped out into the cool dusk air. The sun had set, but pink streaks filled the sky. The neighborhood was end-of-the-day sleepy. She could hear pots clinking from an open kitchen window next to Huey House and the blare of a TV across the street. Streetlamps flickered on as she took her first steps down the street.

The brownstone next to Huey House was labeled with a painted number: 73. June stood before the waist-high gate and looked up. The house was made of gray brick and had big bay windows facing the street. After waiting another few moments, hoping that Tyrell would magically appear, she took a deep breath and went up the thirteen steps. Thirteen was an unlucky number in America—but not in China, she reassured herself. Then she knocked on the door.

THIRTY-TWO
Tyrell

DOWN IN THE BASEMENT CHAPEL, TYRELL SAT on a pew with the mice. He had moved them into a plastic travel aquarium he had found in the shelter's backyard a year ago. MacVillain had confiscated a kid's gecko and thrown the whole aquarium in the trash, gecko and all. Tyrell had tried to find it so he could return it to the kid, but by the time he had, the little lizard was already dead.

Tyrell had cleaned the aquarium and kept it, knowing that it could come in handy one day. The mice scrambled around in the box. He wanted to let them out, but he had to wait for the right time.

"I know how it feels," Tyrell said to them. He looked at his watch. It was getting close to curfew, so he put the aquarium in his bag and headed for the door.

Down the hall, a couple of the cleaning staff were finishing up their shift. Tyrell listened at the door, waiting for them to be done.

"I can't believe we have to come in early tomorrow afternoon for that meeting," he heard one woman say.

Tyrell peeked out the door. The women wore the maintenance uniform: a dark blue T-shirt with the Huey House logo and khaki work pants. They were new employees; he had only seen them around a few times.

"What could be so important?" the other woman grumbled.

"New policy, is what I've heard," the first woman said. "Something about moving families out faster. A guy from the Department of Homeless Services is coming to explain everything."

The second woman whistled. "DHS is coming? Sounds serious."

"At least we're getting overtime."

The women disappeared up the stairs before Tyrell could hear anything else. He stepped back into the chapel, then checked his watch. It was eight fifty-five, and he needed to get upstairs before curfew. After one final check of the hallway, he left the chapel, locking the door behind him.

As he went up the stairs, he wondered how June's lesson

had gone. It had killed him not to go with her. He wanted to meet this violin lady in person more than anything, but the name June had called him a few hours earlier still stung.

Secret: Every time he looked in the mirror, he saw his dad looking back at him.

THIRTY-THREE

June

THE INSTANT JUNE KNOCKED ON THE DOOR, loud barking came from within. The dog sounded very large and very angry.

The door opened a crack, and a woman with black hair woven into hundreds of tiny braids poked her head out. "Hold on," she said before slamming the door in June's face.

June glanced around at the darkening street, then leaned over the banister to peek through the side window. She could see vague shadows moving around behind the lace curtains. There was more barking.

Suddenly the sound quieted. June wondered if she should knock again. Had Domenika forgotten about her? Then something crashed into the other side of the door.

June sprang back and almost toppled down the thirteen stairs. She could hear Domenika yelling inside. Should she give up and go back to Huey House? She was tempted, but she also really needed help if she was to have any hope of getting into the school orchestra.

"Uh . . . Domenika?" she called. "Should I come back later?"

Aggressive snuffling came from inside, then some muttered curses. Finally, silence.

Once more, the door opened a crack. "Sorry," Domenika said, looking twice as annoyed as when she'd first opened the door. "I wasn't expecting anyone." She waved her hand in June's direction. "Well, I mean, Abuela mentioned she was sending me *someone*, but I didn't think it was a *kid*. What's your name, again?" Domenika said. The door was still open just a tiny crack; it did not appear as if she was planning on letting June in.

"I'm June?" June said through the sliver of door.

The door opened wider, revealing a tall woman wearing a long skirt in an African print and a breezy white blouse. She was barefoot, and a pair of spectacles dangled from a chain around her neck.

"First, don't make a statement a question," Domenika said, her voice clipped. "It makes you look unreliable and unprofessional."

She stepped to the side, and June assumed this was her invitation to come in.

If one word sprang to June's mind upon entering the lady's apartment, it was *hoarder*. While the outside of the brownstone was regal and clean, the inside revealed books scattered on the floor, a jumble of shoes—some looking as if they had gotten jammed in a paper shredder—piled by the door, and a crumpled rug, the tasseled edges short in some places and long in others. A garish gold frame surrounding a canvas painted blue with one yellow splatter in the lower right-hand corner hung crookedly on a wall.

Then June glimpsed the animal making the noise. It was huge. Definitely bigger than she was, maybe even bigger than Marcus. Large canine teeth were chomping on what looked like the thighbone of a horse. June backed toward the door, but Domenika had already shut it. Her back hit the solid wood as her hand fumbled behind her for the doorknob.

"That's Bartók," Domenika said in disgust. "He's not mine. I hate dogs. My friend had to leave town to do a concert tour in Europe and left Bartók here when I was buying groceries."

June held her viola case in front of her as a shield.

"Are you going to get your instrument ready or not?" Domenika snapped.

When June didn't move, Domenika rolled her eyes and strode out of the foyer and into the room to their left.

"Bartók won't hurt you," the lady called over her shoulder to June. "That bone will keep him occupied for at least twelve minutes."

June shuffled along the wall, not letting her eyes stray from the "dog."

"What piece are you doing for this audition?" asked Domenika as she dropped onto a couch and swiped at her phone.

"How do you know I have an audition coming up?" June asked. She was positive she hadn't mentioned it to Abuela.

"I don't. This is an audition for *me*. So I can tell if it's worth my time to take you on as a student."

"But Abuela never said anything about auditioning for you."

"Are you playing or not?" Domenika demanded, glaring at her phone, which was pinging and flashing with alarming regularity.

June put her case on the floor and slowly took out her viola. Meanwhile, Domenika reached under the couch and pulled out a battered cardboard box filled with sheet music. After a few seconds of rifling through the contents, she pulled out a yellowed piece of paper and dragged a music stand from the corner of the room and set it in front of June along with the sheet music. "Sight-read this."

June glanced at the notes on the page. She was not a fan of sight-reading. "Wouldn't you rather hear me play the Telemann—"

"This," she said, jabbing a finger at the sheet music.

Taking a moment to tune, June briefly squinted at the lines in front of her. Right away, she could see that this was *not* going to be an easy piece, especially since she hadn't gotten new music to learn in months. Her brain and her fingers seemed to have lost communication with each other. The bow felt heavier than normal, and the second she put it to the strings, it controlled her, skittering over toward the bridge and then toward the fingerboard.

June bit her lip as she struggled through the piece. This was why she didn't play for anyone. This was why she was afraid to see a new teacher. This was why she should have given up playing viola when Dad died. There was no way she could audition for the school orchestra. To her horror, tears filled her eyes.

"That's enough," Domenika said, interrupting June's playing. She paused to check something on her phone, then tossed the device onto a side table. "That was *terrible*," she said flatly. "It *literally* hurt my ears."

June turned her head away and swiped her eyes with a sleeve.

"Being good at anything requires hard work. There are no handouts," Domenika lectured. "To be honest, I don't know if I can work with you. I'll tell Abuela."

"Fine," June said, putting her viola back into its case and zipping it up. "Don't help me. This wasn't even my idea."

Bartók didn't even look up as June burst out the front door and ran back to Huey House, hot tears rolling down her cheeks.

WEDNESDAY, OCTOBER 3

Days at Huey House
Tyrell: 1,278; June: 4

THIRTY-FOUR

Tyrell

THE NEXT DAY AFTER SCHOOL, TYRELL AND Jeremiah jogged back to Huey House. Tyrell had told Jeremiah about his brilliant plan during lunch. So after Tyrell's weekly meeting with Ms. G (Ma didn't show up), they met in the chapel, where Tyrell had stashed the mice. With the aquarium tucked in Tyrell's backpack, they headed back up to the main floor, bumping right into Ms. Jill, MacVillain's assistant. She was weighed down with an armload of files, and startled when she saw them. Jeremiah reached over to help rebalance the papers.

"Where's everyone going?" Tyrell asked.

"Staff meeting," Ms. Jill said.

"Ms. Jill," Tyrell said, walking next to her. "Have I told you how nice you look in that dress?"

Ms. Jill sniffed. "I've known you too long to fall for your charms, young man. And since I haven't attended the meeting yet, I have nothing to report." She hugged the files closer to her chest. "I'll be back in an hour. Don't get in trouble."

Ms. Jill made her way down the stairs to the conference room along with what seemed like every employee at Huey House except for Stephanie, who was tending the front desk. She had her phone out, Tyrell noticed, probably taking the opportunity of not being supervised to call her boyfriend.

"All clear," Tyrell told Jeremiah, and they headed for MacVillain's office.

When they got to her door, Jeremiah slid on gloves. Tyrell rolled his eyes even though he knew fingerprints were the main reason people were found guilty—many years of watching detective shows had taught him that. MacVillain's door was locked, but Jeremiah picked the lock in less than three seconds.

"This lock is insulting," Jeremiah said with disgust as the door clicked open.

They stepped inside and walked to the desk. It was overflowing with papers, folders, and sticky notes.

"What are we looking for?" asked Jeremiah, staring at the mess.

"Any information about the meeting or the new shelter policy," Tyrell told him.

Jeremiah handed him a pair of gloves, and they started sifting through files. There were time sheets and memos and checklists. If she had to look at those papers all day, MacVillain's job must be super boring. Tyrell was about to move on to another pile when he saw a folder labeled APPLICANTS. He scanned a few of the cover letters.

"Hey," he said slowly, holding the folder up and not quite believing what he was seeing. "These are résumés."

"For what?" Jeremiah asked without looking up from the pile he was going through.

"For Ms. G's job."

THIRTY-FIVE

June

WHEN JUNE AND MAYBELLE RETURNED TO HUEY House after the long bus ride from Chinatown, the shelter was oddly silent. Stephanie was examining her nails at the front desk.

"Why is it so quiet?" June asked as she signed in.

Stephanie sighed as if June had asked for a huge favor. "There's a meeting."

Upstairs, June and Maybelle dropped off their backpacks and found Mom in bed again. She didn't stir at their arrival. June left her viola under the bed since it sounded as if Ms. MacMillan was still at Huey House, and then they headed down to the basement.

"Hi, June! Hi, Maybelle!" Lulu said when she saw them.

"Are you helping out today?" June asked.

"There's some big meeting, so Ms. Parveen asked me to fill in this afternoon."

"Maybelle!" Jameel called. "Churro is awake!"

Maybelle dashed to the hamster cage, and the two friends watched as Churro made a rare daytime appearance by scurrying through one of the tubes.

Lulu sat at a tiny table, helping kids with a craft project. "How was your vy-oh-la lesson last night?"

"It wasn't a lesson, it was an audition," June said sadly as she watched the kids squirt glue and glitter all over the table. She didn't even bother correcting Lulu's pronunciation of *viola*.

Lulu paused. "Wait, what?"

"Abuela made it *seem* like it was a lesson, but Domenika treated it like an audition. I wasn't ready, obviously. Guess how many steps lead up to her door?"

"Four?" guessed Lulu.

"Thirteen!"

"So you're superstitious about Chinese *and* American numbers?"

"And now I can't find Tyrell," June said, then explained what had happened the day before.

"He knows this place better than anyone," Lulu said after

she listened to June's story. "If he doesn't want to be found, you can give up on seeing him."

June closed her eyes, defeated. It was strange how only a couple of days could make someone feel like a friend, and she had already managed to lose him.

THIRTY-SIX
Tyrell

TYRELL CHECKED HIS WATCH, SURPRISED AT HOW late it was. He shoved the applicant file into his backpack, behind the aquarium. The mice scrambled around inside, agitated.

"We've got to go!" he told Jeremiah.

Jeremiah nodded, and they headed out of the office, locking the door behind them. The hallway was empty, so they made their way to the conference room. Through the narrow window on the door, they could see that the meeting was still in session. They swung around the corner, where Tyrell knew there was a blind spot from the security cameras, opened a maintenance closet, and slipped inside. In the wall between the back of the closet and the conference room there was a convenient hole, the perfect size for small mice to squeeze through.

Tyrell and Jeremiah created a little barrier around the hole using boxes of cleaning supplies; then Tyrell opened his backpack and pulled out the aquarium. He pried off the top and tipped the container into the small area they had created. As they expected, the mice beelined for the hole.

The second the mice disappeared from view—they were fast!—Tyrell stuffed the aquarium into his backpack, and he and Jeremiah snuck out the door. A minute later they were downstairs in the basement, eating snacks in the cafeteria.

Three minutes later they heard screams.

THIRTY-SEVEN

June

JUNE HEARD SCREAMS ECHO THROUGH THE SHELTER. Lulu ran to the door. Across the hallway, Tyrell and Jeremiah were peeking out from the cafeteria entrance.

"I assume you have something to do with this?" Lulu asked them.

"What's going on?" Tyrell said, eyes wide, the picture of innocence. "We're just having a snack."

The clatter of footsteps down to the basement revealed two men in Huey House uniforms. They jogged past the after-school room, opened a maintenance closet, and emerged with a box.

"What are you doing?" Maybelle asked.

"There are mice in the conference room," one of the men said.

"They came out right as the DHS guy was talking," the other man said. "He screamed and jumped onto the table."

"What are those?" Maybelle said, pointing at the box.

"Mousetraps," the first man said. "Ms. MacMillan hates mice."

The men headed back upstairs, and Maybelle looked at Lulu in panic. "They're going to kill the mice?"

Lulu glared at Tyrell. "Always causing trouble."

Tyrell glanced at Jeremiah. "Let's go upstairs."

June knew she had to talk to Tyrell before he disappeared again, so she took a deep breath and stepped toward him. "Tyrell, I'm really sorry about what I said to you yesterday and even though I've only known you a few days I think you are one of the coolest people I've ever met and you showed me where to practice my viola and you saved it from MacVillain and if you'd tell me what I can do to make you forgive me I would be really grateful."

Tyrell stared at her for a few seconds, then broke into a smile. "I'm one of the coolest people you've ever met?"

"Yes," June said.

"The best-looking, too, right?"

June trained her eye over his right shoulder. "Umm, sure."

Tyrell nodded, satisfied. "Okay, you're forgiven, but *only* if I can come to all your viola lessons with Domenika."

June swallowed. "That might be hard."

"Why?"

"Because I'm not taking lessons. I failed the audition."

Tyrell scoffed. "And you're going to let *that* stop you?"

"Yes?" June said.

"Wrong," Tyrell said. "We're going to find a way to get you those lessons."

"How?"

"I'll think of something. But first, we've got to catch some mice."

THIRTY-EIGHT

Tyrell

IT WAS HARDER TO CATCH MICE THAN it was to release them.

"How many were there?" June asked Tyrell.

"Ten," he said, scanning the now empty conference room, the aquarium open at his feet.

"Got one," Jeremiah said immediately, cornering a tiny white mouse and trapping it under an overturned box.

"Wow," Maybelle said. "You're fast."

There were only two ways for the mice to leave the conference room: through the door or through that little hole that led to the maintenance closet. While Jeremiah and Maybelle took the aquarium and went around to see if any of the mice had returned to the closet, June and Tyrell stayed in the conference room to see if they could catch any.

The door opened, and Marcus poked his head in. "You can't be in here. There's mice."

"We know," Tyrell said. "We're trying to catch them."

Marcus paused. "I don't imagine *you* had anything to do with this?"

"Us?" Tyrell asked. "We're just trying to help."

Marcus narrowed his eyes. "Henry and Jordan already put traps out."

"Maybelle doesn't want them killed," June told him. "Which is why we're trying to catch them."

"She wants to bring them to the park," Tyrell added, "where they can live out their lives with joy and purpose."

"These traps aren't going to kill them," Marcus said.

"Are you sure?" June said.

Marcus nodded. "I'll give them to you once we've caught them all. You can free them in the park."

They followed Marcus out of the conference room and bumped into Maybelle and Jeremiah, who had caught two more mice they had found huddled in the maintenance closet.

"Aren't they so cute?" Maybelle squealed, holding up the aquarium.

Marcus shook his head. "You all are weird."

"Marcus said the traps are humanitarian," Tyrell told Maybelle. "He'll give the rest of the mice to you when he catches them."

"Can we take these to the park now?" Maybelle asked June.

"Sure," she said.

"We'll come with you," Tyrell said. He put the aquarium into his bag and they headed to the lobby. "How was the meeting?" he asked Marcus, who trailed behind them. Marcus was probably making sure they actually took the mice outside.

"Fine," he said.

"Did they say more about the housing program?" Tyrell asked as he opened the security door that led to the lobby.

But Marcus didn't respond. Ms. G was at the front desk, admiring Stephanie's new manicure. When she saw Tyrell, she smiled. Then Marcus appeared, and Stephanie immediately fluffed her hair.

"Hey, Marcus," she said, sitting up straighter and smiling.

"Hey, Stephanie," he said.

Tyrell glanced at Ms. G, but she was busy looking through the logbook.

"Hey, Ms. G," Marcus said, walking over and casually leaning against the security desk next to her.

"Oh, hi," Ms. G said. She was now neatening a stack of job-fair flyers.

A bell rang, and Stephanie checked the security camera

and buzzed the person in. The door to the shelter opened, and in came Ms. Hunter from the birthday party three days ago.

"Iris!" Ms. G said, walking over to give her a hug. "What are you doing here?"

Tyrell followed Ms. G. "Hey, Ms. Hunter."

"Hey, Tyrell," she said, smiling at him. She looked at Jeremiah. "Hey, Jeremiah."

Tyrell was surprised she remembered their names.

"I love your hair," Maybelle said, admiring Ms. Hunter's pink hair. "I'm Maybelle, and this is my sister, June."

"Hi, Maybelle and June. I'm Ms. Hunter."

"What are you doing here?" Ms. G asked again.

"I came to bring these," she said as she pulled a huge box of AA batteries from her backpack and handed them to Ms. G. Then she took out two more boxes—wrapped in bright paper—and handed them to Tyrell and Jeremiah. "And these are for you."

"Do *I* get a gift?" Maybelle asked.

"When's your birthday?" Ms. Hunter asked.

"February."

"I'll remember that," Ms. Hunter said, tapping a finger to her temple.

"You already gave us a birthday present," Tyrell said. He looked at Jeremiah, who shrugged, and they ripped open the paper. Inside were Yankees caps, and not imitation ones either. He could tell because they had the silver visor sticker and a neatly embroidered label inside that said GENUINE MERCHANDISE.

"Wow," Tyrell said as he put his on. It fit perfectly.

"I made my best guess for the size, so if they don't fit I kept the receipts—"

"They're perfect," Tyrell and Jeremiah said at the same time.

Ms. Hunter gave a sigh of relief. "I'm glad you like them. And I didn't forget these . . ." She handed them each a bag.

Tyrell looked inside. "Ugh, books?"

"Nice," Jeremiah said, smiling. "Thanks, Ms. Hunter."

"You're very welcome," she said. Then she noticed Marcus and stepped over to him. "Hi, I'm Iris Hunter. Ms. G's friend."

"I'm so sorry," Ms. G said, flustered. "I should have introduced you two."

"I'm Marcus," Marcus said, shaking Ms. Hunter's hand.

"Oh, *you're* Marcus," Ms. Hunter said, smiling. "I've heard all about you."

Marcus raised his eyebrows. Ms. G's face turned scarlet.

"Iris, want to grab a coffee?" Ms. G asked, suddenly in a rush. "There's a great place right by the subway station."

"Sure," Ms. Hunter said, then looked at Marcus. "Nice to finally meet you."

"Same," Marcus said before Ms. G hooked elbows with her friend and pulled her out the door.

"Wow," June said as she watched them leave. "That was so nice of Ms. Hunter."

"I'm going to ask her for a hamster just like Churro for my birthday," Maybelle declared.

"Marcus, what are you doing this weekend?" Stephanie said, focusing her heavily mascaraed eyes on Marcus.

Marcus looked at Stephanie. "You know, the usual. Working on my bike. Dinner with my ma." He glanced at his watch, then at Tyrell. "I've got to finish my shift and head home. Don't forget to take that"—he pointed to his backpack—"outside."

As Tyrell signed himself out, Stephanie examined her nails.

"One day he'll ask me out," she informed him.

Tyrell nodded, but as they walked out the door, he thought, *I don't think so.*

❡

The mouse release, which Tyrell had thought would be a quick task, turned out to be a big event. Tyrell and Jeremiah led June and Maybelle to Bill Rainey Park, down the street from Huey House. It had baseball diamonds and a football field. Big trees along the perimeter of the park created shady walkways.

"This is really nice," June said.

Maybelle looked around, her eyes wide. "This is like a vacation spot for mice!"

As they walked along the path, Jeremiah suggested areas to release the mice and Maybelle rejected every idea.

"It has to be perfect," she told him, scrutinizing each square foot of the park as if the mouse-release location were the most important decision she would ever make. Suddenly she stopped and June bumped into her.

"Right there!" Maybelle said, pointing to a grove of trees near some huge rocks. A little cluster of purple flowers grew out of the rocky ground.

Tyrell unzipped his backpack and took out the aquarium. He was about to pop open the top when Jeremiah stopped him.

"I feel like we should pray over them or something," Jeremiah said.

"That's ridiculous," Tyrell said.

"Great idea!" Maybelle said.

Tyrell sighed.

Maybelle squeezed her eyes tight and clasped her hands. "Please, God, watch over these little mice and let them be happy here in their new home. They are so little and really need you to protect them."

Tyrell was surprised to feel his eyes burn, but he blinked the sting away.

"Are you ready *now?*" he said, glancing at his watch. When Maybelle, June, and Jeremiah nodded, he opened the top and handed the aquarium to Maybelle. She gently tipped it, and after a moment of stunned realization, the three mice ran out, disappearing underneath a bush.

"Freedom," Jeremiah said as he watched them go.

What Tyrell *wanted* to say to Jeremiah was *What's so great about freedom? What if they can't find food? What if other animals eat them? What if they freeze in the winter?*

What Tyrell said instead was "I hope they make it."

"They will," Jeremiah replied.

There was something about Jeremiah's confidence that made Tyrell feel suddenly uncomfortable. He shoved the aquarium back into his backpack, the container getting caught in the folder of résumés. He pulled the papers out, walked to a nearby trash can, and tossed them in. Maybelle was watching the spot where the mice had been released, but they had vanished, off to build their homes and find food and keep from being eaten and survive in the wild all by themselves.

Tyrell pulled his Yankees cap lower onto his head and looked at Jeremiah and June. They had taken a seat on a wood bench under an enormous tree with wide, arching branches. Maybelle crouched by the purple flowers, watching a line of ants disappear into a crack between the concrete path and the soil. A light breeze moved through the trees, making the dry autumn leaves rustle. Across the way, a woman had a cart full of tamales for sale. When she opened the top of the cart to select some for a customer, a rich, spicy smell drifted in their direction.

Tyrell wanted to freeze time. Things were good right now, but why did he have a sinking feeling that they wouldn't stay that way for long?

THIRTY-NINE

June

AFTER A DINNER OF MORE SQUARE VEGETABLES and stale bread rolls, June got ready to put Maybelle to bed. As they went upstairs, Tyrell told June that he would meet her outside her door at eight o'clock.

"This is part of your plan to get me back into viola lessons, isn't it?" she asked him.

"Heck yeah," Tyrell said. "I want to meet that lady."

"She's a dragon," June told him. "A fire-breathing dragon with a werewolf for a pet."

"She has a dog?" Maybelle asked, listening in on their conversation. "I want to meet the dog."

"No one is going to meet her or her dog," June told them. "Because I'm not going back there ever again."

"I'm picking you up at eight," Tyrell said. "Trust me."

And she remembered when Tyrell had said "trust me" the day before. "Okay, fine," she said. "But we're not going next door, I don't care what you say."

June and Maybelle continued upstairs, and June used her key to let them into the room. Mom was in bed, as usual. June left an apple and a bread roll on the nightstand next to her, then got Maybelle changed into her pajamas. They brushed their teeth together, and June pulled back the covers so her sister could climb into bed.

"Lullaby," Maybelle demanded as she set up her stuffed animals in their preferred sleeping positions.

"I'm tired today," June told her.

"Please?" Maybelle said.

June sighed but leaned down and got her viola case from under her bed. When she lifted it out, she saw the sheet music from the previous day's "lesson" pressed at the bottom of the case. It must have fallen inside in her haste to leave.

June left the music where it was and took out her rubber mute instead. She fit the mute over the wooden bridge, which muffled the sound. As Maybelle snuggled deep into the covers, June lifted the viola and set it between her shoulder and chin.

She played a different piece today—"Rêve d'enfant" by Eugene Ysaÿe, which was one of her favorites—even though Maybelle preferred Brahms. After a few moments of playing, her mother shifted in her bed so that she faced them. She didn't open her eyes, but a smile played on her lips. Both of her parents used to love when June played. Sometimes when she was practicing, they would stop what they were doing and listen to her.

A tiny speck of hope bloomed in June's heart but fizzled immediately when she remembered where they were. After playing the last hopeful notes of "Rêve d'enfant," June played "Berceuse" by Amy Beach, its notes casting a spell of peacefulness throughout the room and making her forget for one moment where she was. By the time she finished the piece, Maybelle was asleep. June wanted to keep playing—it was the first moment of serenity that day—but it was getting close to eight o'clock. She packed up her viola, put it under her bed, and opened the door to find Tyrell and Jeremiah leaning against the wall.

"This way," Tyrell said, walking down the hall. When they passed the stairwell, Jeremiah peeled off.

"Gotta talk to my mom," he said, detouring to the stairs.

"He doesn't like classical music," Tyrell told her as Jeremiah disappeared.

June nodded. "Not that many people do."

"I like it," Tyrell said. "It makes me feel calm."

Tyrell headed to the opposite end of the hallway, and to June's surprise there was an alcove tucked into the wall right by the window. She had never walked in that direction and had not noticed it before.

Tyrell sat down on one side of the wide windowsill and immediately took out his homework. June settled down next to him, feeling awkward.

"What are we doing here?" she asked.

Tyrell tilted his head toward the window. "Shh . . . I think it's starting."

June leaned against the window. The familiar sounds of tuning filled her ears. While June loved the viola and its rich chocolate notes, she also adored that high violin string that rang so perfectly.

It had been a long time since June had heard music played by someone so good. Domenika's violin sounded like a babbling brook, then like thunder, then like birds in the early morning, then like church bells.

After listening for thirty minutes, June got off the windowsill and headed down the hall toward her room.

"You're leaving already?" Tyrell said, disappointed.

"I need to practice," June called over her shoulder. "Domenika is never going to take me as a student if I don't."

THURSDAY, OCTOBER 4

Days at Huey House
Tyrell: 1,279; June: 5

FORTY
Tyrell

THE NEXT DAY AFTER SCHOOL, TYRELL AND Jeremiah found a notice taped to the front door of the shelter.

COMMUNITY MEETING TONIGHT
5 PM IN CAFETERIA
ATTENDANCE MANDATORY

They glanced at each other, then raced up the stairs to the lobby.

"What's with the community meeting?" Tyrell asked at the security desk.

Stephanie gave a disinterested shrug. "How do I know?

By the way, Ms. G wants to see you," she said, pointing a long fingernail at Tyrell; then, "Sign in with your *real* name."

"Why does Ms. G want to see me? Is it about the meeting?"

"I don't know anything about a meeting. She left a note saying you should go to her office. You're probably in trouble. Again."

"I had my family meeting yesterday," Tyrell protested.

Stephanie picked up her phone and ignored him.

"Good luck, man," Jeremiah muttered under his breath as they parted in the lobby. "Let me know what she says."

Tyrell went down the hall to Ms. G's office. Her door was wide open, so he walked in.

"What's up with the community meeting, Ms. G?" he asked.

"Hello, Tyrell," Ms. G said with a warm smile, getting up from her chair and walking around her desk. "Nice to see you. How's everything going?"

Tyrell raised his eyebrows and did not budge from his spot by the door. "What are you not telling me?"

Ms. G sat on the edge of her desk as she avoided his question. "I remember when you first came here. There was something special about you, and I noticed it right away."

He squinted. "You say that to everyone."

"We've had some great times together. But change is not

always bad. Change is what keeps the Earth rotating, the seasons moving from autumn to winter to spring to summer—"

"Do you have a point?" he interrupted. He didn't like the way she talked about change as if it were a good thing, as if it were something to look forward to.

"Manners, Tyrell," Ms. G said mildly. "You've grown a lot since you got here. I'm really proud of the man you're becoming. And that's all I wanted to tell you."

"That's it? I thought you were going to say something about the community meeting."

"Ms. MacMillan is running that meeting. You'll have to see what she says."

"Is the meeting about the new housing policy? Because I heard—"

"You'll find out soon enough," Ms. G said in her *that's final* voice. "There's another reason I called you in here." Ms. G plucked a bag off her desk and handed it to him. "Fried chicken from Kennedy's. All dark meat. You're welcome."

"Ms. G, I could marry you," Tyrell said, reaching right into the greasy bag, pulling out a drumstick, and taking a bite. The skin was crispy and salty. Perfect.

"Aw, you're so sweet," she said. "Now, before you leave, tell me about the mice."

Tyrell choked on his drumstick, and Ms. G handed him

a glass of water and waited patiently while he gulped some down. She wore her *I'll wait as long as it takes* face. But Tyrell knew better than to admit anything, so he picked up his chicken again and took another bite.

Ms. G sighed. "When the DHS guy saw the mice, he jumped on the table and screamed so loud I thought a mouse had gone up his pants leg."

"I'd like to have seen that."

Ms. G raised her eyebrows, so he changed the topic before she could question him further. "What's the deal with Marcus? I think he totally digs you."

Ms. G frowned. "Marcus? We're just friends."

It was Tyrell's turn to raise *his* eyebrows. "You get all flustered around him, and you're *never* like that with anyone else. You've got it bad."

"Nope," Ms. G said.

"C'mon, Ms. G. What's the holdup?"

"I have all you little troublemakers to keep track of. Who has time for a relationship?"

"But Marcus is amazing. Who are you waiting for? Barack Obama and Lin-Manuel Miranda are already taken."

Ms. G laughed.

"You're lucky," Tyrell said, peeling a piece of chicken skin off another drumstick, "because I have suggestions for how you can show him you're interested. First, you need to actually smile and talk to him instead of running away whenever he comes near."

"I don't think—"

"Next, you need to ask him questions. How will you get to know him if you don't ask him questions? And no talking about work."

"Work is the only thing we have in common—"

"Wrong," he said. "You're both great with kids. You both love reading. Ooh, you can ask if he's read any good books lately!"

"Tyrell—"

"Do it," he told her. "It's good for your character."

"I think you've spent too much time around me," Ms. G said, making a face at him. "You're making such reasonable points. I regret being such a good social worker." She went back around her desk and sat down. "Now let's get back to *you*. I know something is up. You have a look in your eyes. Anything you want to tell me?"

"No."

"Really?"

"Really."

"Really?"

"C'mon, Ms. G. Can't you let a guy enjoy his chicken in peace?"

FORTY-ONE
June

THE BUS RETURNED TO HUEY HOUSE, LATE as usual, and June noticed the sign on the door of the shelter right away.

COMMUNITY MEETING TONIGHT
5 PM IN CAFETERIA
ATTENDANCE MANDATORY

She checked her watch. It was 4:55.

"Come on, Maybelle," June said, grabbing her sister's wrist. She signed in and Stephanie buzzed them into the main building. They raced downstairs to the cafeteria, which they found overflowing with people. Given the noise level, June figured the meeting hadn't started yet. Maybelle squeezed past people and disappeared into the cafeteria, and June had no choice but to follow. Maybelle settled down at a table with Tyrell and Jeremiah, who scooted over to make room.

Ms. MacMillan coughed, and when it was reasonably quiet she began.

"As you might have heard, there are a record number of homeless people living in New York City." Her voice was flat as she addressed them. She stood in front of the hot-food bar wearing what looked like a brown potato sack with nylon stockings and boring brown leather shoes. Next to Ms. Mac-Millan was a man in a droopy suit with pants legs puddling at his ankles. He wore spectacles so round they made him look perpetually surprised and he was exactly the same height as Ms. MacMillan. His eyes scanned the ground as if there were something fascinating down by his feet.

"As a result," MacVillain continued, "the Department of Homeless Services is implementing Housing Stability Plus, a program that provides short-term rental vouchers to move people out of shelters and into housing. The plan is to free up shelter space for more homeless families who are entering the system."

A sudden burst of exclamations buzzed through the cafeteria.

Ms. MacMillan raised her voice to make herself heard. "The Department of Homeless Services has sent us a housing specialist to help with the transition. This is Mr. Fernsby."

The man next to Ms. MacMillan raised his head. He wheezed as he spoke. "I'm—*heh*—Mr. Fernsby. You—*heh*—can contact me anytime. My—*heh*—office is next to—*heh*—Ms. MacMillan's. Thank you."

There was a stunned silence, then a bluster of shouts and questions.

Lulu's mom's voice rose above the rest. "Does this mean we have to leave immediately? Ms. Gonzalez has me in a job training program. I want to finish it before I leave."

"Where can these vouchers be used? I've heard they're only for dangerous neighborhoods!" another woman called out.

Then Tyrell stood up and looked straight into Ms. Mac-Millan's eyes. "I heard there's a new rule about getting us out of here within ninety days."

There was a hushed silence; then a roar rose in the cafeteria.

"Quiet! Order!" Ms. MacMillan glared at Tyrell. "There is no official policy."

"But I heard they were going to give you money if you got us out of here in ninety—"

Ms. MacMillan raised her voice again to drown out Tyrell. "In the case of the vouchers, they can be used in many different areas throughout the city. Mr. Fernsby will walk you through all the specifics during your housing appointments next week. Please honor your appointment times, as rescheduling is difficult." With that proclamation, Ms. MacMillan walked briskly out of the cafeteria, Mr. Fernsby shuffling behind her.

The meeting had been three minutes long and dinner wouldn't begin until six o'clock, but people stuck around the cafeteria. June could almost see their minds turning as they thought about how this would affect them. Moms and grandmothers talked quietly, trying to keep their troubles from the kids.

"I'm not letting that Fernsby man decide where I live," one said. "Did you see that article about the places they put homeless families?"

"Old motels way far away from everything," another said.

"Horrible school districts."

"Crime everywhere. Gangs."

"Not even near subways. To get decent work you'd have to commute for hours every day."

"Buildings no one wants to live in."

"Drugs. Guns."

June looked around and wasn't surprised to see that her mom wasn't there. While all these women were thinking about how the policy would affect their kids and families and work, Mom couldn't even bother to come downstairs.

June was left to figure things out on her own. Again.

FORTY-TWO
Tyrell

TYRELL SAW THE EXACT MOMENT JUNE LOOKED around the room and realized her mom wasn't there. It wasn't as if Tyrell's mom was mom of the year or anything, but at least she was here. Of course, they did shut off the television in the community room during the meeting, giving her nothing else to do. Tyrell had never even seen June's mom, and that said a lot since he knew practically everyone at Huey House.

He wasn't sure what to say to her, but then Lulu and Ms. Vega came over.

"June!" Ms. Vega said, embracing June and giving her a kiss on each cheek. June made the classic mistake of turning her head to avoid the kissing, and Lulu's mom's lips caught June's ear instead, leaving a smudge of pink lipstick.

"This has been a terrible day, and I think we all need pampering!" Lulu's mom said, rubbing June's long locks between her index finger and thumb. "Your hair would be so cute with some layers and a blowout with a nice round brush. What do you think?" Then Ms. Vega whipped out a fashion magazine and flipped to a page where a leggy model in a flimsy sundress looked out at them with a pouty mouth, her hair flying around her face in what they wanted you to think was wind but what Tyrell knew was an industrial fan.

"That model is my exact opposite," June announced, and Tyrell nodded in agreement. "I look *nothing* like that." She pointed to her ponytail. "See this hairstyle? I've had it like this for the last eight years. I think my hair is permanently dented where the rubber band holds it together."

"But, honey, use your *imagination*. This"—Ms. Vega pointed to the magazine—"could be what your hair looks like."

Tyrell squinted at the magazine, but the model and June really looked so different. He wasn't sure if Ms. Vega could pull it off.

"You don't have to do it," Lulu advised June. "It's your hair."

"Come on, June," Ms. Vega pleaded. "I need more practice hours so I can get my license. I'm running out of time."

There was a long pause; then June closed her eyes and nodded. "I'll be there after I put Maybelle to sleep."

"I want to go too!" Maybelle protested.

"You can't," June replied flatly.

Maybelle grumbled, but then someone Tyrell had never met before entered the cafeteria. Was this June's mysterious mom?

"Um, June?" Tyrell said, poking June's elbow.

"What?" June said.

He nodded toward the woman, who was making her way across the room.

June lowered her eyes to the table.

"Jèhjè," June's mom said when she reached their table.

The people around them had gone silent.

June had never said anything about her mom — or her dad, now that Tyrell thought about it — and he wondered why.

June stood up. Maybelle stood up as well, glancing warily between her mom and her sister.

Then June looked Ms. Vega in the eye. "I'm ready for my haircut now."

FORTY-THREE

June

NO ONE SAID A WORD AS JUNE made her way upstairs with Ms. Vega, Lulu, Maybelle, Tyrell, and Jeremiah. When they got to the fourth floor, Lulu opened her door and pointed to a chair. June sat down and yanked out her hair tie.

"I was thinking of keeping it nice and long, just trimming some of the ends and then doing a light layering. Sound good?" Lulu's mom suggested.

"Fine," June said flatly. "Do whatever you want."

Ms. Vega paused for a moment, then said, "Honey, I don't know what happened between you and your mom. But I want to share a little secret with you: People are not perfect. We all make mistakes, even mothers."

June nodded, but she didn't say anything. It did not make

her feel better to hear that all people made mistakes. Her mother had done more than make a mistake. She had abandoned her family.

She had abandoned *June.*

"Families are complicated," Ms. Vega continued. "But remember that it does not cost you to be open to forgiveness."

June was not in the mood to get a lecture about forgiveness, because forgiveness was exactly what Mom *didn't* need. Mom needed to take care of her daughters, but no one seemed to be giving *her* lectures.

Ms. Vega picked up the scissors. When she was about to cut, Abuela took that exact moment to fling open the door and shout, "What were you *thinking* ruining your *one* chance with Domenika!"

June heard Ms. Vega say something in Spanish, a word that did not sound good; then she saw a hunk of hair on the ground.

"Oy!" Abuela said, her hands flying to her mouth.

"Don't panic," Lulu said in what June perceived to be a very panicked voice.

June reached up slowly and touched her hair. There was a considerable amount missing on the left side, above her ear.

"That's . . . not good," Tyrell said.

June turned to look at her friends. Tyrell and Jeremiah were leaning against the wall by the door, and their mouths twitched, as if laughter was begging to be let out. Standing up, June walked to the mirror.

"Listen, muñeca," Ms. Vega began, the tips of her polished nails tapping against each other. "I can fix it. Don't you worry!"

It was bad. Really, really bad. A hunk of hair was no longer there. Instead, jagged edges stuck out in multiple directions.

To no one's surprise, Tyrell cracked the chilly atmosphere. It started with a wheeze, then graduated to gasps, and finally ended up in booms of laughter that echoed off the walls.

"I'm sorry!" He gasped. "You—should ask—for—your —money back," he managed to say between the laughs, his hands holding his sides.

June watched everyone exchange looks. Ms. Vega was silently pleading with Abuela to help her out. Abuela was looking up at the ceiling and moving her lips in what June assumed was a prayer. Tyrell was bent over, still cackling, and Jeremiah had turned around to face the wall but his shoulders shook with laughter.

June glared at Tyrell and Jeremiah. "I'm going to sneak into your room in the middle of the night and shave half of your head and you can see how it feels."

That only made Tyrell laugh harder.

FORTY-FOUR
Tyrell

TYRELL SUGGESTED TO JUNE THAT SHE MIGHT not want to confront Domenika with her hair looking the way it did, but she just shook her head and looked more determined. Ms. Vega had tried to fix the hair catastrophe, but in the end, they decided to shave that section off since it was so jagged and close to the scalp. On the other side of June's head—the area where the hair remained long since June had refused to let her even trim it—Ms. Vega had put her hair into a French braid, so June looked like some kind of bizarre Brooklyn hipster/indie musician.

After her hair was fixed, June grabbed her viola and went downstairs with Tyrell. Stephanie was so involved in picking at her chipped nail polish that she didn't look up when they signed out, which was good because June was in the zone. She was intent on confronting Domenika, and nothing was going to stop her.

At ten minutes before eight o'clock, June marched up the thirteen steps to Domenika's door. She rang the bell. Inside, a creature started barking as if the world were ending. Tyrell glanced at June, but her eyes were trained on the door. A loud *whomp* startled him. The front door shuddered with the impact.

"Maybe this wasn't such a great idea," Tyrell said.

"Domenika!" June yelled, banging on the door with her fist. "I've got something to say to you."

The door didn't open, but he could see the curtains covering the window to the left of the door flutter slightly. June noticed it too.

"I know you're in there!" June yelled as she leaned down and opened her viola case. "Come out here!"

Tyrell looked around. The street was quiet, but the thought that some neighbors might call the police on them made him uneasy. "June, I don't think she wants to see you."

June glared at him as she pulled her viola and bow out. "What happened to never giving up? Fighting for what you want?"

"I was wrong?"

"I want Domenika to teach me—and you, too, I know you want to learn—and I'm not stopping until she says yes."

And with that proclamation, June lifted her viola and played a piece so beautiful that if he hadn't been watching her with his own eyes, he would have thought it was Domenika playing. All the while, June's words echoed over and over in his ears. *I know you want to learn.*

And the truth was, Tyrell *did* want to learn. He wanted to one day be able to pick up an instrument and play music like June and Domenika. But no one else had ever looked at him and said, "Hey, Tyrell, you look as if you would make a fine violin player."

None of the violinists he had ever seen looked like him, with his brown skin and hair buzzed at the sides and sticking straight up at the top. None of them lived in the Bronx, in a homeless shelter. Tyrell might not know much about classical music, but he knew music lessons took money and a parent who cared.

When June had the viola in her hand, it looked as if it were a part of her. He didn't want her to stop playing, but her music slowed and the last note drifted out into the universe.

The neighborhood was quiet.

June brought her viola down from her shoulder.

The door before them did not open.

FRIDAY, OCTOBER 5

Days at Huey House
Tyrell: 1,280; June: 6

FORTY-FIVE

June

THE NEXT MORNING, JUNE AND MAYBELLE WERE standing in front of Huey House at five twenty-five, waiting for the school bus. June's eyes felt gritty from not getting much sleep. Everyone was staring at her hair.

A little finger poked at her arm, and June looked down.

"Why is your hair shaved off right there?" Jameel asked, pointing at the left side of her head.

"You look weird," added Shania, a second grader who June recognized from the after-school program.

"*I* like it," Maybelle said defensively. "I want to get my hair cut like that too."

The bus pulled up. "Hey, munchkins, you ready to roll or

what?" yelled Charlie as he cranked open the door. Everyone piled in. Marcus waved from the street.

Halfway down the block, Charlie hit the brakes. The older kids braced themselves against the seats in front of them, and some of the little kids slid off the seats and fell into a giggling heap on the floor. Why the bus didn't have seat belts, June had no idea. She heard the doors squeak open, then a woman's voice. It was a voice she vaguely recognized.

"Who's that?" Maybelle asked, leaning into the aisle and trying to glimpse the new person.

June stilled. The voice grew louder. "No," she whispered.

"She looks mad," Maybelle said.

June shrank down into her seat. "It's Domenika."

"Who's Domenika?"

"The violin lady!" June hissed. "Hide me!"

Domenika made her way down the aisle, right toward them. June sank lower in her seat. To her surprise, Domenika didn't glance at them. She took the empty seat in front of them instead. Jameel and Shania were in the seats across the aisle from her, and they stared at her long, braided hair in wonder.

"Is that *real* hair?" asked Shania. "Have you been growing it since you were a baby?"

"I got extensions," Domenika replied.

"Wow," Jameel and Shania breathed.

Then the bus started moving and everyone sat there, staring at Domenika. June could only see the back of her head. Twenty minutes later, when she had decided that the woman had boarded the bus only to confuse and torture her, Domenika turned around and passed her a folded piece of paper. June considered not reaching for it, but curiosity overwhelmed her. She unfolded the paper. The note was written on musical staff paper, and Domenika had used the staff as lines to write on.

I know I can be a jerk, the note read.

June considered that for a moment before digging a pen out of her backpack.

Yes, June wrote, then dropped the paper over the top of the seat into Domenika's lap.

Domenika glanced at the note, then wrote something and passed it back.

I'll give you a chance if you give me a chance.

June scribbled back. *Did Abuela put you up to this?*

Domenika stood and turned around, her hands holding the back of the seat for balance, her dark eyes looking right into June's. "I do have a conscience. Also, what happened to your hair?"

June didn't say anything.

Domenika gritted her teeth. "I'm standing on a school bus

that smells like armpits at six in the morning. I would be very grateful if you forgave me so I can go back home. How long do you ride this thing, anyways?"

"About two hours," June said.

Domenika tsked. "All that practice time, wasted." She looked around the bus. "You should use the commute time to practice. Of course, you have to be very careful not to drop your viola."

June stared at her. Maybelle looked back and forth between them, as if she were watching a table tennis game.

"Just a suggestion. You can do some finger-strengthening exercises, at least," Domenika said with a shrug. "If I'm going to teach you, I expect you to practice. A lot."

"Wait. What are you saying?" June asked.

"Come to my place tonight at seven."

"You're really taking me on? It's not an audition?"

"Be there. Be ready."

"How do you know *I* still want to work with you?"

Domenika looked surprised. "You don't want to?"

"I do," she said. Then she thought about Tyrell and the way he looked when he watched her practice. "But I have a condition."

Domenika raised an eyebrow.

"You also teach my friend Tyrell. He's a big fan. He listens to you practice every day at eight o'clock. He's been listening for years."

"Really?" Domenika said.

June nodded. "So, do we have a deal?"

"What piece is Tyrell working on?"

"He doesn't play at all. But I can help him."

Domenika sighed. "I don't teach beginners. Most of my students are in high school and college. They're preparing for conservatory or on their way to be professional musicians."

June knew she had to say something to convince Domenika to take him as a student. "Come on. He's lived in a shelter for three years. He's always wanted to play but he's never had an opportunity."

The bus crawled down the avenue, cars honking all around them as a cab tried to cut across three lanes of traffic. June waited.

Finally, Domenika nodded. "Okay, but you both better practice like your lives depend on it or I'm dropping you. I don't care what Abuela says."

"Okay," June said, trying to keep the smile from spreading across her face.

"You're going to practice before you see me?"

"Of course! Geez."

"I'm coming too," Maybelle said. "You have a dog, right?"

"It's not my dog," Domenika said. "And he's a monster. Now I've got to get off this bus. How can you stand the smell?"

June watched Domenika lurch down the aisle to the front of the bus and talk to the driver. Charlie veered to a corner by a subway stop and let her out. Everyone on the bus scooted to the right side so they could watch her walk down the sidewalk, descend the subway station stairs, and disappear underground.

"Are you really going to practice on the bus?" Maybelle asked when they settled back into their seats.

June didn't respond. She was already pulling out her viola

FORTY-SIX
Tyrell

AFTER SCHOOL, TYRELL AND JEREMIAH SAT IN the chapel. While Tyrell was supposed to be working on his social studies homework, Jeremiah read a book for extra credit. Tyrell was also doing his best to distract his friend. He wanted to cruise around Huey House looking for more information about this Housing Stability Plus policy, even though Marcus and Ms. G had both said they had none.

Tyrell sighed loudly, paced up and down in front of Jeremiah, and eventually started throwing lime-green jelly beans at him. Jeremiah had marvelous concentration skills, though. He had no problem ignoring his friend.

The sound of someone entering the chapel made them both drop to the ground and roll under the pews. Jeremiah got jammed halfway in, but then Tyrell caught sight of June and her viola.

"What are you guys doing?" June asked, nudging his leg with her foot.

"We thought you were MacVillain," Tyrell said, emerging from beneath the pew.

"Not such a great hiding place, dummies," June said. She put her viola case on the pew and said, "Isn't life amazing?"

"Oh boy," Tyrell said. "What happened to put you in such a good mood?"

"Domenika changed her mind," June said, pausing for effect. "She's going to teach me."

Tyrell grinned even as his stomach dropped. Had June asked about him?

"That's great," he said.

June gave him a look. "I said no."

"What?" Tyrell and Jeremiah said.

"I said I wouldn't do it unless she took you as a student too," June said to Tyrell. "And she said she didn't teach beginners, and *I* told her that you were going to practice a lot and finally she said yes and our first lesson is today at seven o'clock," she finished.

Tyrell blinked. "What did you just say?"

"She's going to give you lessons," June repeated. "And I'm going to help you practice."

"Seriously?"

"Seriously. And you have to do everything I say, because I know more about music than you do."

Tyrell got up and approached her.

"You *do* want lessons, right?" she asked.

"I've wanted lessons my whole entire life," Tyrell told her. Then he grabbed her in an unexpected hug and didn't let go until she pounded on his back with her fists.

FORTY-SEVEN

June

WHILE JUNE HELPED TYRELL PRACTICE PUTTING HER viola on his shoulder and holding it the right way, they talked about the new housing policy.

"We've got to stop it," Tyrell said. "MacVillain didn't say anything about the ninety days, but I know it's happening. I heard those HQ suits talking about it. Can you imagine what will happen if we actually have to leave in three months?"

"Isn't it a policy from city government?" Jeremiah asked. "How can we change that?"

"Maybe the time frame is a good thing," June mused as she helped Tyrell adjust the instrument closer to his neck. "I mean, who wants to stay here forever?"

"Not everyone is ready to leave," Tyrell said. "Jeremiah

and I have been here for three and a half years. Have you seen my mom? She can't hold a job for longer than a week."

June thought about what Tyrell had said. "I understand about your mom, Tyrell. My mom is a total mess. I had to do everything on my own before we got here. Grocery shopping, cooking, taking care of Maybelle. At least here we have food and a place to live. Maybelle is happy and has friends."

"We have Marcus and Ms. G," Tyrell added. "And we have each other."

And all of a sudden, June remembered that second day here, when she had walked in on Jeremiah's meeting with Ms. G. Was he still moving soon? If he was, it didn't seem as though he had told Tyrell. She glanced over at Jeremiah, but his face was calm and inscrutable as ever. *That guy should play poker*, she thought.

Tyrell continued talking. "From what I overheard, once this new idea is in place, HQ gets extra money if families are booted out within ninety days. Ms. G doesn't like the new policy, and I heard the HQ people say that MacVillain should get rid of her. And yesterday, we found a stack of résumés for a new family services director."

"Get rid of Ms. G?" June said. "But she's amazing."

"I know," Tyrell said.

"What did you do with the résumés?"

"Threw them away," he said.

"Maybe we can talk to politicians," June said. "Write letters or something. Who's that mayor guy of the Bronx?"

"Bronx Borough President Sanchez," Jeremiah said.

"Yeah, him," Tyrell said. "He did some kind of filming here a couple of years ago for the news. I think his office gave Huey House a big grant or something."

"That's perfect," June said, pulling out her notebook. "He already has a connection to this place."

"Jeremiah, you could change all the locks at the Department of Homeless Services offices so no one can do any work," Tyrell said.

"No," Jeremiah said.

"You could hack into their computer system," Tyrell suggested.

"Nope," Jeremiah said.

They continued to throw out ideas until they heard people coming down to the basement for dinner. So they snuck out of the chapel, picked up Maybelle, and had a quick dinner.

Then it was time for June and Tyrell to have their first lesson with Domenika.

FORTY-EIGHT
Tyrell

TYRELL HAD LOVED CLASSICAL MUSIC EVER SINCE second grade, when his teacher had ended most school days with a read-aloud. While she read, she would play classical music from her computer. She was the best teacher Tyrell had ever had.

Following June and Maybelle out of Huey House, Tyrell was astonished that he was actually going to have a lesson. Most of all, he couldn't believe June was willing to put her own lessons on the line so he could learn how to play.

They went up the thirteen steps to Domenika's brownstone and braced themselves for the inevitable barking when June rang the doorbell. After a few moments of frenzied sounds on the other side of the door, Domenika appeared. The first thing Tyrell noticed was her skin color, which was as dark as his. Long braids trailed down her back.

"Tyrell?" Domenika asked, looking at him.

He nodded.

"I'm Maybelle," Maybelle said before Domenika could ask. "You were on our bus this morning."

"Come in," Domenika said, opening the door wider.

Maybelle was the first one through the door, and she bee-lined for the hugest dog Tyrell had ever seen in his life. It had long curly hair and a big mouth dripping with drool.

"That's Bartók. I put him on a leash," Domenika said. "Don't approach unless you want to be knocked over."

Maybelle, of course, approached.

"Oh, hello, Bartók," Maybelle said, dropping to the ground in front of him and stroking his enormous forehead. "Who's the sweetest dog in the world? I just want to take you home!"

Tyrell watched in amazement as Bartók collapsed—the whole brownstone shuddered when he hit the floor—and rolled onto his back, exposing his huge belly.

"Wow," Domenika said. "That's . . . unusual."

"I've watched a lot of dog training videos," Maybelle informed her. "For when I get Nana."

"I'm going to hire you to babysit him," Domenika said. "He's never this quiet."

"I'll do it for free," Maybelle said.

Tyrell couldn't let *that* happen. "She charges twenty dollars an hour."

Domenika leveled a stare at him. "Five."

"Fifteen," he countered.

"She'll take five," June said, glaring at Tyrell.

"Five whole dollars for hanging out with you!" Maybelle said to Bartók. "Can you believe our luck?"

"Come on, we don't want to waste the whole hour staring at Bartók. Get your instruments out," Domenika said.

"Tyrell doesn't have an instrument yet, so he can just use mine," June said.

Tyrell sucked in a breath. He knew how protective she was of her instrument.

Domenika shook her head. "He needs a *violin*, not a viola." Marching into her living room, she pulled open a closet door. There were clothes hanging from a rod and boxes crammed inside and even a Bartók-sized teddy bear. Domenika shoved things aside until she pulled out a violin case.

"This should do," she said, setting it on the coffee table and unlatching it. She took it out, held it horizontal in front of Tyrell, and nodded. She then put it to her shoulder and played a few notes. She fiddled with the knobs until the sound was as bright and clear as the most perfect autumn morning. Then she handed it to Tyrell.

"That's for me?" he asked, not daring to move. "You're kidding, right?"

"It's just sitting in there, gathering dust," Domenika said with a wave of her hand. "I don't even know why I have it. We'll probably need to put new strings on it and rehair the bow soon, but it will work for now."

Tyrell stared at the violin, admiring the beautiful wood and how it curved in the middle and the way the f-holes swirled elegantly on either side.

"Don't just stand there holding it," Domenika said. "Put it on your shoulder. Let's make sure it's the right fit."

Domenika had him hold the violin between his shoulder and chin. The violin curved into his body as if it had been made for him.

"Now carefully extend your arm and *don't drop the violin*."

Tyrell made sure the violin was nestled firmly under his chin before extending his arm.

Domenika stepped back. "That fits you perfectly. Okay, here's the bow. I trust June already taught you how to hold it?"

"Yes," he said.

"Good. June, are you paying attention? You have to pay attention during his lessons or you won't be able to practice with him later."

"I'm paying attention," June said.

Domenika showed him how to stand and how to put the

bow on the violin and how to extend and bend his right arm to make sure the bow stayed straight. By the end of thirty minutes, he felt exhausted. There was so much to think about.

"That's enough," Domenika said. "June, tune up. It's your turn."

"I didn't know just playing one note involved so many steps," Tyrell said. "It looks easy when other people do it."

Domenika sifted through a stack of music on a dresser. "Every musician starts where you are. My goal is to set you up right so we don't have to break bad habits later. Practice that arm extension and the straight bow and make sure the pinkie on your bow hand is curved." She looked at June. "Okay?"

"Got it," June said, tuning her viola.

Tyrell nestled the violin—*his* violin!—into its case and strapped it in using the dark blue velvet tabs. Then he loosened the bow and put that in the case as well, gently closing the lid and latching it. He double-checked that he had latched it right. He didn't want the violin falling out.

As he listened to June and Domenika working together, Tyrell kept putting his hand on the case just to make sure it was still there. No one had ever given him something so beautiful.

After one lesson, Tyrell had a whole new appreciation for how good June was. She made everything so musical, even though he knew that it wasn't easy to make such a pretty sound. When he had tried, the bow had screeched against the strings.

"We're done for today," Domenika said, looking at her watch.

It was almost eight o'clock.

"Are you going to practice now?" Tyrell asked her.

"Yes," she said. "Leave me alone."

"Can we come back tomorrow?" June asked her.

Domenika sighed. "Most teachers only teach once a week, *and* they get paid. I'm actually losing money since I'm giving Maybelle five dollars for hanging out with Bartók."

"So we can come tomorrow?" June asked.

Tyrell admired her persistence.

"Fine," Domenika said. "But you can't come every day, okay? I have a life. And only come if you've practiced a lot, okay?"

Maybelle reluctantly got up from where she had been brushing Bartók and murmuring stories to him. All around were tumbleweeds of Bartók's fur.

"Look how great he looks," Maybelle said, gesturing to him as if she were showing off a car on one of those game shows that Ma liked to watch in the mornings. Dog hair clung to Maybelle's clothes. Bartók sneezed, and hair flew everywhere.

Domenika sighed. "I guess I should vacuum."

They left as Domenika turned on the vacuum, the roar of

the motor almost drowning out Bartók's sad howls at Maybelle's departure. When they got back to Huey House, Stephanie looked at their instrument cases with squinty eyes.

"What are *those?*" she asked, pointing her sharp nails at them.

"Backpacks," Tyrell said. "It's the new fashion."

Marcus intercepted them as they entered the hallway.

"Don't tell me you have an instrument too," he said. "Ms. MacMillan is going to flip out."

"We're going to be real careful," Tyrell promised.

Marcus gave him a look. "Maybe keep that downstairs."

Tyrell nodded. There was no way he was bringing the violin into his bedroom. Last year, he had won an iPod from the New York Public Library's summer reading program. Anyone enrolled had gotten a raffle ticket, and when his number was called, he could not believe his luck. When he showed the brand-new, still-in-its-case iPod to Ma, she smiled and said it looked nice, and the next day he couldn't find it anywhere even though he was sure he had put it under his pillow.

Ma had gone missing the rest of the day, and when she came back she had a new pair of shoes even though she hadn't held down a job in months.

It wasn't hard to guess what happened to his iPod, and he was not going to make the same mistake twice.

SATURDAY, OCTOBER 6

Days at Huey House
Tyrell: 1,281; June: 7

FORTY-NINE

June

THE NICE THING ABOUT SATURDAY WAS NOT having to wake up at five o'clock in the morning. The bad thing about Saturday was having to avoid Mom for a whole weekend. The other bad thing about Saturday was that Ms. Gonzalez had set up a meeting with her. It surprised June to find out that it was just going to be her, not Mom or Maybelle, which made her think that Ms. Gonzalez wanted to pry into her feelings.

After June's dad died, a guidance counselor at school, an elderly woman who wore sweaters she knit herself, had pulled June out of class. She peppered June with questions like "How does that make you feel?" and "What is your plan going forward?" and "How can you change a negative into a positive?"

Then the sweater lady had filled out forms while June sat there, silent.

Ms. Gonzalez's office door was open, but June knocked anyway.

"Hey there, June," Ms. Gonzalez said. "Thanks for coming by."

Ms. Gonzalez's voice was very soothing, and she smelled like lilacs again. But why was she here on a Saturday? Did she not take the weekends off?

"So, June," Ms. Gonzalez said. "What's up? Do you like cookies? Because I made raspberry jam cookies last night, and someone needs to help me eat them or I'll eat 'em all myself." She pulled out a thin plate with scalloped edges from her desk drawer and piled fat cookies onto it from a round container the size of those gallon buckets of ice cream.

June didn't respond, but Ms. Gonzalez didn't look annoyed or even concerned. She put the cookies on the coffee table in front of the giant purple couch. June stood there, waiting for her to get to the point.

Ms. Gonzalez picked up a cookie and took a big bite. She closed her eyes as she ate it, as if savoring every mouthful. June's stomach rumbled, and after watching Ms. Gonzalez take another bite, June gave in and snatched a cookie off the plate.

"Grab a seat if you want," Ms. Gonzalez said, motioning to the couch.

Sitting down on the purple couch, June bit into the cookie. It filled her mouth with flavors: sweet raspberry and buttery dough.

"Holy smokes," June said after she had swallowed. "You're wasting your life as a social worker."

Ms. Gonzalez winked. "Anyone's heart can be softened with a cookie. An important life lesson," she said. "Hey, Abuela told me you started lessons with Domenika. That's so cool."

"Tyrell is doing lessons too."

"I'm so glad," Ms. Gonzalez said. "I've been wondering something. When your mom was here yesterday, she referred to you by a different name."

June's mouth dropped open. "You met with my mom and she *talked* to you?"

"Well, I brought a translator in," Ms. Gonzalez said. "I got lucky. The translator was from the same region of China your mom grew up in, so I think that made your mom more comfortable."

June shook her head, disbelieving. "Well, she never talks to *me*. Her only word in weeks was jèhjè. Lulu's mom calls her amor and muñeca."

"What does jèhjè mean?"

"Big sister," June said.

"Maybe that's an endearment in itself?" Ms. Gonzalez asked.

June paused and picked at a thread coming loose from the couch cushion. "I don't think so."

"To me it asks the question of what it means to have a little sister. And what do you think it means to her?" Ms. Gonzalez got up and walked around her desk. She pulled out a drawer and removed a plastic ziplock bag, then dumped the rest of the cookies inside the bag. "I have two siblings, an older brother and a younger sister. Sometimes I get really mad at them. But when my temper cools down a bit, I think about them being family, about us being connected forever. The same blood running through our bodies. The same story drawing us together like an invisible thread."

"But don't you think words matter too?" June asked. She thought about how Mom had never said *I love you*. Was it a Chinese thing? She had talked about it with Eugene once, and he thought Chinese parents show their love through actions, like making food, rather than words. But Mom's actions hadn't been showing love either, so June didn't know what to think anymore.

"I know it's been a hard time," Ms. Gonzalez said, "and I agree that words matter." She sealed the ziplock bag and handed it to June along with another bag.

"What's this?" June asked.

Ms. Gonzalez just smiled and ushered her out the door. "Thanks for stopping by, June. I'm glad we had a chance to talk."

On her way back to her room, June peeked into the second bag. Inside were char siu bao, steamed pork buns. It was her favorite food; she had told Ms. Gonzalez so at their first meeting. June put her nose into the bag and breathed in. It smelled just like home. Dad had always brought a bag of char siu bao on the weekends, the smell waking her up every Sunday morning. Where had Ms. Gonzalez managed to find these?

As she went up the stairs to pick up Maybelle for lunch, June realized that Ms. Gonzalez had not asked one question June had expected her to ask.

FIFTY

Tyrell

WHEN HE COULD, JEREMIAH LIKED TO DO his weekend homework on Saturday mornings. Tyrell preferred to save it until Sunday night, but June had a meeting with Ms. G and he had nothing to do until she could help him practice the violin.

So after breakfast on Saturday, Tyrell and Jeremiah went up to Jeremiah's room and read the next chapter of *Roll of Thunder, Hear My Cry*.

They were up to the sixth chapter, the part when Uncle Hammer appears. Tyrell liked Uncle Hammer. While they read, he could hear noises from life at Huey House: a baby wailing, someone talking on the phone, and the whir of a building fan unit. Then the door opened and Jeremiah's mom stepped into the room.

"Hey, Ms. Jones," Tyrell said.

"Hi, honey," Jeremiah's mom said as she threw her bag on the bed. Then she looked at Jeremiah. "My boss is letting me do the late shift today. I thought you could come with me to the store and choose a few things for your new bedroom. What do you think? Good idea?"

Jeremiah froze. The air stilled.

"What's going on?" Tyrell asked, his voice quiet.

Ms. Jones's eyes widened at the same time Jeremiah's eyes closed.

"Are you *moving?*"

"Oh, honey," Ms. Jones said to Jeremiah. "You were supposed to tell him. We're leaving tomorrow!"

Tyrell stared at his best friend. "Tomorrow?"

Jeremiah looked up and nodded. "I tried to tell you a thousand times."

Ms. Jones reached for Tyrell. "I'm sorry, Tyrell. Everything is going to be just fine."

Tyrell jerked out of her arms and pointed a finger at Jeremiah. "You promised." Then he walked out of the room and did not look back.

9

All of Huey House thought Mamo was a terrible cook and the meanest employee at Huey House, but only one of those things was true. Sometimes when Tyrell was in a bad way, she let him come into the kitchen and peel potatoes.

The potato peeling had started just after he arrived at the shelter three and a half years ago, when his new third-grade teacher at P.S. 511 told his mom that he might have to repeat the grade. Tyrell had just started at the new school and couldn't believe he would have to do third grade all over again. Mamo found him in the basement ripping up the community announcements on the bulletin board, told him to quit it, and dragged him into the kitchen.

Tyrell thought she was going to stab him with one of her kitchen knives. Instead, she gave him a peeler and a twenty-pound bag of potatoes, and now when he experienced that out-of-control feeling he would head to the kitchen.

Mamo didn't look surprised when Tyrell arrived. She pointed to the butcher block table, where a mound of potatoes was waiting.

He peeled in silence for half an hour before Mamo said anything.

"Everything okay?" she asked, her voice gruff.

He looked up from the potato mountain. "Jeremiah's moving."

Mamo nodded. "I heard about that."

That only made Tyrell madder. He ran the peeler against

the potato with a vengeance. "I guess I'm the last to know, huh?"

Mamo shook her head. "I just happened to walk into Ms. MacMillan's office when Ms. Gonzalez was giving an update on the families moving out."

Jeremiah was leaving. The hurt flooded though Tyrell's body again. He continued swiping at the potatoes, a rhythm he had perfected a couple of years ago. Swipe, swivel potato, swipe, swivel potato. Repeat thousands of times. The potato peels overflowed from their metal bowl.

Mamo took down a wooden spoon that could easily have doubled as a shovel and stuck it into a pot that looked like a cauldron. Then she blew out a big breath and ran a handkerchief over her forehead. "I learned to cook when I was eight years old."

Tyrell looked up. Mamo had never once shared something personal during the three years he had worked in her kitchen.

"My mom worked as a prep cook at one of the big hotels on Oahu in Hawaii. When she got the job, they scheduled her for the lunch and dinner shifts, so I was in charge of cooking for my siblings at home."

Imagining Mamo as a little girl was as hard as imagining himself as a grown man.

"I got pretty good at making food without meat because

my little sister was like that Yang kid. You know, the one who had a breakdown at dinner the other day." Mamo paused. "I guess I can try to remember some of those old recipes."

Mamo turned the burner off under the cauldron and dried her hands with the towel that hung from her apron string. Tyrell picked up the last spud, and a few swipes later, the potatoes were done.

"It's a good thing for Jeremiah and his mom, you know," Mamo said. "They're ready to leave. Everyone has to leave sometime."

Tyrell didn't respond. It wasn't just the leaving, it was the lying. For years they had promised to be brothers, to always stick together, to live at Huey House until they were eighteen and then get a place together.

The broken promise was the worst betrayal of all.

SUNDAY, OCTOBER 7

Days at Huey House
Tyrell: 1,282; June: 8

FIFTY-ONE

June

JUNE HADN'T SEEN TYRELL IN TWO DAYS, not since their first lesson with Domenika. He hadn't shown up to their second lesson the night before, which Domenika was not pleased about.

Tyrell had vanished. It was only when June ran into Jeremiah that she found out the reason behind Tyrell's disappearance: Jeremiah was moving.

"You weren't the one to tell Tyrell about the move?" June asked Jeremiah.

"No. He found out from my mom."

Jeremiah looked so awful that June didn't want to tell him her first thought: *I don't know what he's going to do without you.*

"I'm glad you're here," Jeremiah said. "At least he has you."

June thought about Tyrell and all the good and not-so-good parts of him. They had only known each other for a week; Jeremiah had had over three years with him. There was still a long list of things that June didn't know about Tyrell and things he didn't know about her.

On Sunday morning, with Tyrell still missing in action, June stayed with Jeremiah as he packed the last of his meager belongings. Jeremiah kept looking toward the door as if Tyrell would come walking through with a huge smile on his face. They had dropped by his room a couple of times, but he wasn't there, and his mom was no help. Marcus and the other staff hadn't seen him either.

And then June remembered what Lulu had said: if Tyrell didn't want to be found, he wouldn't be found.

Done with their packing, Jeremiah and his mom carried their bags outside to the front of Huey House. June stood on the sidewalk along with two dozen others, waiting to see him off. She watched as Jeremiah put Ms. Gonzalez's gifts—a tub of cookies and a new set of measuring cups—carefully into his backpack.

"Humberto is going to drive you to your new home in the van," Ms. Gonzalez told them when she helped them bring their three bags to the curb. Her eyes were bright with tears. "Be sure to keep in touch. Call or visit anytime."

Jeremiah's mom was wearing a navy-blue dress and looked

happy and terrified and sad at the same time. "I can't thank you enough for everything you've done," she told Ms. Gonzalez as they hugged.

"I'm incredibly proud of both of you," Ms. Gonzalez responded, bringing Jeremiah into the hug.

When they separated, Jeremiah went around to everyone waiting to say goodbye to him: Abuela and Lulu and Ms. Vega and Marcus.

June felt sick as she watched the goodbyes, knowing that the person he most wanted to say goodbye to wasn't there.

A van pulled into the No Standing zone in front of Huey House. Humberto waved from inside.

Suddenly, Jeremiah turned to Ms. Gonzalez. "I've got to do one last thing." Then he looked at June. "Come with me?"

They ran back into Huey House, signed in, and were buzzed into the building. June followed Jeremiah up to the third floor to knock on Tyrell's door and then to the fourth floor to check the alcove, then down to the basement, where Jeremiah quickly picked the lock to the chapel and peeked in.

Tyrell didn't want to be found.

Defeated, they walked back up the stairs to the lobby. Jeremiah signed out one final time; then he went down the stairs and out the shelter doors.

A light breeze fluttered through the air and feathered the tree leaves. A gaggle of kids in soccer uniforms walked by with their coach. Marcus leaned against the side of the van, arms crossed over his chest. Humberto, in the driver's seat, was moving his head and torso to the rhythm of the van radio. Jeremiah's mom was already in the van.

"Do good in this world," Marcus said to Jeremiah, cuffing him on the shoulder. "You have my number. Call anytime."

Jeremiah nodded and climbed into the van. Marcus pulled the door closed behind him. Humberto turned the key in the ignition as he sang along with the mariachi music.

"Can you tell me what the lyrics say?" June asked Abuela as they all watched the van move down the street.

" 'Si usted puede sacarme, con usted yo me voy,' " Abuela said. " 'If you can get me out, I'll leave with you.' "

Marcus and Ms. G stepped out onto the quiet street and waved until the van turned the corner and disappeared from sight.

" 'Tan luego se vio libre, ¡Volo, volo y volo!' " Abuela said. " 'As soon as she saw herself free, she flew, flew, flew!' "

MONDAY, OCTOBER 8

Days at Huey House
Tyrell: 1,283; June: 9

FIFTY-TWO
Tyrell

MONDAY WAS A BAD BEGINNING AFTER A terrible weekend. Tyrell hadn't finished his homework, and Ms. Gruber made sure everyone in his class knew it. Meanwhile, Jeremiah's seat sat empty.

He ate lunch alone—he had never bothered to make friends other than Jeremiah—and the day stretched endlessly before him.

After Tyrell walked home by himself, he dropped his backpack off in his room, grateful that Ma wasn't around. He flopped down on his bed, his hand reaching behind his pillow by habit to pull out the framed photo of him and Jeremiah. He stared at it. Their arms were slung around each other as they laughed at something Marcus was doing.

Tyrell stood up and shoved the photo to the bottom of an old duffel bag he kept under his bed. He didn't want to see that photo ever again.

Not wanting to stay in the room any longer, Tyrell made his way down to the ground floor using a narrow, rarely used staircase at the back of the building. It was rumored to be infested with rodents, so most people steered clear of it. The staircase didn't bother Tyrell. After all, he was the one who had made up the rumor in the first place.

The staircase went down to the hallway right by Ms. G's office, where there was an emergency exit that led to the street. He wasn't supposed to use it. Everyone was told to sign in and out on the clipboard and use the lobby doors each time (Rule 12.3.5), but Tyrell didn't care. When he passed Ms. G's door, it was cracked open and he heard MacVillain's voice.

"We need a family services director who is on board with the new HQ policies and the new direction of the Department of Homeless Services," MacVillain said.

Tyrell paused, standing against the wall just next to the cracked door so he could listen in.

"While I don't agree with this new policy," Ms. G replied, "I would like to continue advocating for these families and guiding them to opportunities while they *are* here. There are many families on the verge of being independent for the long term, and I'd like to see them through to job security and permanent housing."

There was a pause and a rustle of paper. "Unfortunately, HQ has decided that the focus should be solely on housing rather than services. You have openly opposed these priorities, so today will be your last day. You will be paid for the next two weeks."

The darkness already hanging over Tyrell threatened to engulf him. After Jeremiah's leaving, losing Ms. G was too much to bear.

Ms. G's voice was determined. "Moving these families out without jobs or any type of security is a wrong move. Think about what's best for the kids."

"HQ has already passed the paperwork to human resources. Please be ready to give all your client files to Mr. Fernsby and have your personal items removed by end of day. I can give you the necessary forms to continue your health care coverage until you get another job." There was the scrape of a chair being pushed back, and Tyrell disappeared out the emergency side door before MacVillain saw him.

His feet automatically took him in the direction of school, but instead of making a right at the corner, he took a left and didn't stop.

For hours, Tyrell walked aimlessly, weaving in and out of

streets, not even trying to make sure he knew how to get back to Huey House. He eventually found that he had wandered into a familiar neighborhood. Baychester was only a few miles away from the South Bronx neighborhood Huey House was located in, but it was more industrial and less loved. Broken beer bottles and cigarette butts filled empty tree pits, abandoned cars rusted in abandoned lots, and barbed wire lined the top of the fences. He slowed when a cluster of forty-story red-brick buildings emerged from a street filled with warehouses and car repair lots—these were the projects he had grown up in, the one-room apartment where there was never enough food, where he had slept on the couch. The buildings were taller than he remembered. Emptier and lonelier.

This was the place he came from, the place he kept hidden from even his closest friends. June and Jeremiah would never understand what it was like to see their father's mug shot in the newspapers. They would never understand how people in his old neighborhood had looked at him, and the way they'd stopped answering the door when he came looking for someone to play with. They wouldn't understand what it felt like to get a letter from their dad with the return address of a state prison.

He continued walking, as if pulled by a force. He knew exactly where the store was, even though he had never been inside in all the years he had lived in the neighborhood. Ten minutes later, he stood before a bodega squeezed between Rite Check Cashing and AJ Wine and Liquor. The door was open, and he walked back and forth along the sidewalk and sneaked peeks into the bodega each time he passed. It was a narrow shop, with only one aisle that went all the way to the back and shelves overflowing with canned food, toilet paper, and cleaning supplies. A man — the storekeeper — was behind a counter shielded by bulletproof glass.

On his third walk by the store, he noticed a small altar on the sidewalk by the front door. His heart clamored in his chest as he stared at a laminated photo taped to a candle in a tall glass painted with the Virgin Mary. A flame flickered inside, the wick halfway burned down and the inside of the glass coated with soot.

Then Tyrell saw the rumpled sign underneath the photo.

BOLÍVAR ORTIZ
Beloved Father, Husband, and Friend
February 26, 2015
Vaya Con Dios

He read it again, and again, and then a third time. He knelt down and stared at the photo. The man in the picture had a big smile and dark eyes that sparkled. He was looking off to one side, and his eyes shone with pride at whatever — or whoever—he was looking at. Tyrell reached a hand out to touch the man's face.

"Hey, kid."

Tyrell looked up, and the man coming out of the bodega stopped in his tracks. He knew what the man saw. Because on the night that his father had shot and killed Bolívar Ortiz, another man had been working in the store. A guy who was lucky to be behind the bulletproof glass and not restocking the soft drinks. A man who had seen everything, including his father's face.

A kid Tyrell's age came out of the store. "Tío? I'm done stocking. Do you need anything else?"

The kid saw Tyrell too, and Tyrell knew that the kid was Bolívar's son.

He scrambled up. The older man held out his hands and started to say something, but Tyrell didn't wait to hear it. He ran down the street and did not look back.

The man shouted something to him.

Tyrell kept running.

MONDAY, OCTOBER 22

Days at Huey House
Tyrell: 1,297; June: 23

FIFTY-THREE

June

THE WEATHER TURNED COOLER OVER THE NEXT two weeks, churning deeper into October and autumn. The leaves shed their green in favor of yellow and orange and burgundy, transforming their normally monochrome street into a more inviting, cozy avenue. The shelter received a van full of donations, and June and Lulu spent an afternoon picking through it for winter clothes for the after-school kids. Four trailers had been installed in the backyard, and families had already been moved in. The cafeteria was getting crowded, and arguments were breaking out over the one television in the community room.

The past two weeks had been a time of mourning for everyone. Jeremiah was gone. Ms. Gonzalez's office was cleared.

News flew around the shelter saying that Ms. MacMillan had fired her. A few residents had seen her being escorted off the premises by a new security employee. Now, instead of weekly meetings on Ms. G's puffy purple couch with cookies warmed by steaming cups of tea, the families sat in cold metal folding chairs in Mr. Fernsby's office and filled out endless forms.

The day after Jeremiah moved out, there had been a big commotion because no one had seen Tyrell since he had left for school that morning. Police were called, Marcus walked every street in the South Bronx looking for him, and Humberto drove slowly around the neighborhood. Tyrell's mom had been utterly unfazed by his disappearance. He had finally come back at nine thirty that night with holes in the knees of his jeans and a haunted look in his eyes.

The next day, he acted as if nothing had happened. Whenever June asked about it, he changed the topic. His already thin frame ventured into gauntness.

They had had six lessons with Domenika and they practiced together every day. Tyrell was improving remarkably. The violin seemed made for him, and he picked up the music naturally, as if all those years of listening to Domenika practice had seeped into his bones. It was hard for June not to feel jealous at how easily it came to him. And while Tyrell didn't talk about Jeremiah or Ms. Gonzalez, June could hear his feelings coming out in his playing. The notes had a yearning in them that went right to her heart.

Maybelle continued to go to Domenika's with June and Tyrell so she could hang out with Bartók. She had earned thirty dollars so far, which she saved in a jar for Nana's future supplies, and every day Maybelle would nag June to take her to the animal shelter. June didn't know how to make that happen. She wasn't certain she could figure out how to get to the shelter from Huey House, and besides that, she was exhausted from the long commutes to school and hours of practice every day.

To make everything worse, there was no word from Jeremiah. No phone calls. No emails.

The letters they had written to Bronx Borough President Sanchez and a handful of other politicians and officials at the Department of Homeless Services two weeks earlier about the unfair housing policies went unanswered. They used the shelter phone to call 311, New York City's information hotline, but they were given information for the Emergency Assistance Unit, not the DHS offices they requested.

June was worried. It had already been a couple of weeks since Mr. Fernsby had arrived, and everyone was anxiously waiting to hear how the new policies would affect them. June had always imagined she would move back to Chinatown eventually, but how could she be sure? Everyone at Huey House was on edge.

On Monday evening in late October, June headed for Domenika's house with Tyrell and Maybelle for a lesson. They had been going earlier, right after dinner, so Maybelle could be in bed by seven thirty. June's audition for the school orchestra was scheduled for the next day, and Domenika wanted to make sure she was 150 percent prepared. When they arrived, they let themselves in without knocking. Bartók crashed through the brownstone at the sound of their arrival, skidding to a stop at Maybelle's feet and sitting on his haunches.

"June, you go first," yelled Domenika from the other room. "I need to hear your audition piece."

June unpacked her viola, tuned, and warmed up with scales. When she had finished playing her audition piece, Maybelle and Tyrell applauded, but Domenika yelled, "You've been working on intonation, right? Because it doesn't sound like it."

Domenika emerged from the kitchen and sat down at the piano. They went through the first half of the piece with Domenika playing the piano while June played her viola, trying to match the tone of each note.

When progress had been made, Domenika worked with June on different phrases and advised her on how to make them more musical. After half an hour, she sent June to practice in the basement while she worked with Tyrell.

June expected the basement to look like something out of a horror film. Instead, it was carpeted, with two comfortable armchairs and a colorful rug on the floor. Two large bookshelves contained musical scores, and framed photos hung on the wall. Looking closer at some of the photos, June spotted one that stood out from the rest: Domenika was playing the violin for the president! Of the United States! There was another photo where she was onstage at Carnegie Hall's Stern Auditorium with a full orchestra behind her. She had on a beautiful red gown and stood right next to the conductor. June took in a sharp breath.

The person teaching her was famous.

♩

June practiced until Domenika yelled for her. She took one last look at the photos and headed up. Maybelle was sitting by the stairs, Bartók drooling on her shoulder.

"Look, I've taught him a new trick," Maybelle told June. "Bartók, are you tired?"

Bartók immediately opened his mouth wide, showing them his big teeth. It looked as if he could use a good dental cleaning.

"I'm practicing all these tricks on Bartók so when we get Nana she can learn them too. We're going to visit her soon, right?" Maybelle asked.

"Yeah, sure," June lied, not wanting to create a scene at Domenika's house.

"For your audition," Domenika said when she saw June, "remember to do a nice easy shift to fifth position in bar eighty-three, okay? And get that finger firmly on the string. I don't want you to make that screechy sound."

"Yeah, yeah," June said as she bumped her viola case against her leg.

"What time is the audition?" Domenika asked.

"Ten."

"You'll be fine. But for goodness' sake, think about your intonation! And your rhythm! Remember, you need to *sing* measure forty-eight!"

Tyrell packed up his violin and headed for the door.

"Bye, Bartók," Maybelle said. "I love you."

"See you later, Domenika," June said. "Thank you."

Domenika ushered them outside. "Have a good audition or I'll give you more scales and études," she said, closing the door in their faces before June could respond.

She stared at the door, then looked at Tyrell. They burst into laughter while Maybelle yanked at their hands and yelled, "What's so funny? *Tell me!*"

But, as often happened those days, the laughter didn't last long. When they reached Huey House, they found Marcus standing at the doorway watching a boy and a woman get into a car.

Maybelle ran toward the vehicle. "Jameel!"

"Maybelle! Come back!" June yelled, running after her.

By the time Maybelle reached the curb, the vehicle was pulling away. June could see Jameel's face and hands pressed against the glass.

"Jameel!" Maybelle screamed, running down the sidewalk until the car picked up speed and disappeared into the evening.

Marcus caught up with her and pulled her into a hug even though she elbowed him in the stomach in her fury.

"His mom disappeared last night," he said. "ACS had to take custody of him."

ACS was the Administration for Children's Services, the city agency that operated foster homes.

"He can stay here with us!" Maybelle cried. "I can take care of him!"

Marcus hugged her even tighter. "Oh, Maybelle. The system doesn't work that way. We didn't have a choice."

"I'm sorry, Maybelle," June said, watching helplessly, knowing words were useless.

Maybelle didn't seem to hear. She wormed free from Marcus's hug and pummeled his chest. "You let them take him away! You let them take him away!"

Marcus let her hit him, over and over again, until she finally stopped fighting and collapsed in his arms. He pulled her into a fierce hug.

"I didn't get to say goodbye," Maybelle said against his chest, tears streaming down her face. "I never get to say goodbye."

June shivered. Maybelle hadn't gotten to say goodbye, not to Dad, or to Nana, or to Jameel. The people and animals she loved were taken away from her without notice.

And there was nothing June could do to bring them back.

FIFTY-FOUR

Tyrell

THERE WERE A LOT OF SAD ENDINGS at Huey House, Tyrell thought as he watched Jameel leave the shelter with strangers. It reminded him that what had happened to Jameel could easily happen to him. It was only because of Ms. G and Marcus that he and his mother were still here, and now the future seemed more uncertain than ever with Ms. G gone.

After June calmed Maybelle down and put her to bed, she met Tyrell in the chapel. They took turns practicing, June helping him with his bow hand and making sure the notes were right. At eight thirty, there was a knock on the door.

"Should we hide?" June whispered, alarmed.

"Nah," Tyrell said, and he went over and opened the door.

Outside were Marcus, Abuela, Lulu, and Ms. Vega.

"We're here for the concert," Abuela said, pushing her way in and sitting herself down in a front pew. She looked at June expectantly.

"What?" June asked.

Tyrell closed the door behind them and turned to June. "Thought you might want some practice before the big audition."

June glared at him. "I don't."

Marcus smiled as he settled down next to Abuela. "Come on. I paid big money for these tickets."

"I'm not ready to perform for you," June told them.

"You better get ready quick, because your audition is tomorrow!" Ms. Vega said.

"We're going to love it," Lulu told her. "Especially since we don't know anything about violin."

"It's viola!" June said, exasperated.

Tyrell looked at June. "You can't disappoint your fans."

June sighed. "I'll only play if you play something too."

"Sure," Tyrell said, then looked at his friends. "But don't expect much. I only started a few weeks ago."

June put her viola on her shoulder.

"What are you playing?" Abuela said.

June sighed again. "Viola Concerto in G Major by Telemann."

"Louder!" Abuela said. "Head up! Look like you know what you're doing!"

"June, dear, you need to project confidence," Ms. Vega said. "Here is something Ms. G taught me: Stand and reach your hands up to the ceiling. Pretend you're six feet tall."

"Ha," June said, but she put her viola down on a table and reached up. "I feel stupid."

"Here," Tyrell said. "I'll do it with you." And he proceeded to puff up his chest and reach toward the ceiling as if he were a superhero getting ready to save the world.

"There!" Abuela said, pointing at Tyrell. "Do it like that, June."

June looked at him and rolled her eyes but tried to imitate him, nonetheless.

"Perfect!" cried Abuela.

"Hold it there!" Lulu said.

"You already look like a winner!" Marcus declared.

After fifteen seconds, Ms. Vega said, "Now introduce your song again, June."

June stood up straight, looked at her audience, and said in a loud, clear voice, "I will be playing the fourth movement of Georg Philipp Telemann's Viola Concerto in G Major."

"Woohoo!" Lulu called.

Tyrell watched June lift her viola onto her shoulder and

proceed to play the piece as well as he had ever heard her. The quick notes darted through the chapel, making everything lighter and livelier. After she was done, they gave her a raucous round of applause complete with whistles and cheers.

June grinned. "I've never gotten that reaction after a recital performance!"

"Get used to it," Marcus said. "We're coming to all your concerts, and we're going to be that annoying family that makes a lot of noise."

June smiled, then turned to Tyrell. "Your turn."

"Fine, but it's sort of embarrassing to play after you." He picked up his violin and carefully put it on his shoulder. "I will be playing Allegro by Shinchi Suzuki."

Allegro means *lively.* Tyrell did what he could, using his charm to make up for his mediocre violin skills. When he finished thirty seconds later, the audience erupted again.

"Aww," Tyrell said, touched at their reaction. "June was a million times better."

"You are a natural, Tyrell," Abuela said.

"I'm glad you're playing the violin," Marcus said, "although I'm trying not to be offended that you would rather do this than play the djembe drum."

"I like hearing *you* play the drum," Tyrell told him.

The concert over, Marcus, Abuela, Lulu, and Ms. Vega

headed to the door while Tyrell and June packed up their instruments.

"Remember," Ms. Vega said to June before she left. "Stand up tall and be proud of who you are."

The chapel turned quiet again, and Tyrell carefully wiped down his violin with a soft cloth before nestling it into the case.

"Are you mad at me for inviting them?" he asked.

"No," June said. "It was actually really nice. Thank you."

"You're going to rock that audition," Tyrell said with complete confidence.

He stood up like a superhero, chest puffed out and arms overhead.

June imitated him, and they both burst out laughing.

"Ms. Vega," Tyrell said, shaking his head as they walked out of the chapel. "She has the strangest ideas."

TUESDAY, OCTOBER 23

Days at Huey House
Tyrell: 1,298; June: 24

FIFTY-FIVE

June

JUNE WAS READY FOR HER AUDITION. RIGHT before her turn, she did Ms. Vega's weird superhero pose before walking into the auditorium and performing the heck out of her Telemann viola concerto.

The orchestra list was posted on the hallway bulletin board after school. June rushed over right after dismissal. Next to the list of violists was her name, plus a note: *Viola Soloist*. Her stomach jumped at the sight. She was the soloist!

June was so pumped with adrenaline that she didn't notice Maybelle wasn't waiting by the bus as usual. When she boarded and Charlie asked where her sister was, a wave of panic rolled through her body. They both got off the bus and looked around.

Charlie flagged down one of the teachers from the elementary school to ask for help while June scanned the crowd of kids. There was no sign of Maybelle. Charlie pulled out his phone to call the shelter to see if she had gone home on an earlier bus. June ran through the scenarios in her mind: Maybelle had gotten sick and gone to the doctor. She had a thing after school and she had forgotten to tell June. She had to use the bathroom.

Then June saw the school police officer jogging toward them.

FIFTY-SIX
Tyrell

TYRELL SAT IN THE HUEY HOUSE LOBBY, passing time before June got back from school. While life seemed to go on as normal—he ate his meals in the cafeteria, went to school each day, signed in and out of Huey House using the same old clipboard—nothing felt right.

He missed Jeremiah and Ms. G.

Really missed them.

Tyrell hadn't caused a stir in Huey House for weeks now. Even Maria Castro had stopped darting away when he passed by, although she did still carry her rosary beads and whispered prayers at the sight of him. The thing was, Tyrell didn't care anymore.

The phone rang at the security desk, and Stephanie picked it up. She immediately tapped on the glass of Marcus's office and gestured for him to come out. Marcus grabbed the phone.

"She just didn't show up?" he said, his voice laced with worry.

Pause.

"Okay, I'm leaving right now."

He looked over at Tyrell. "Maybelle didn't show up at the school bus this afternoon."

Marcus took out his cell phone and pressed a few buttons. "Humberto, can you get the van ready? We need to go to Chinatown."

❦

There was no way Tyrell was going to hang back at the shelter while Maybelle was missing. She could be lost. A kidnapper could have lured her into his car, promising her a puppy or a three-legged hamster. He sprinted outside, Stephanie yelling at him to come back, and scrambled into Humberto's van and buckled himself in. When Marcus rushed out of Huey House a few minutes later, Tyrell could tell he was considering whether it was worth prying him out of the vehicle. In the end, Marcus left him alone. Ten seconds later, Mrs. Yang emerged from the shelter, ran to the van, and climbed in next to him. As they sped down the street, she kept turning her wedding ring around on her finger, over and over again.

Tyrell had not spent much time with Mrs. Yang. June rarely talked about her. Recently, Maybelle had been coming down to the cafeteria for dinner with her mom, but he'd never had a conversation with her. She didn't seem like the kind of person who wanted to be social.

As Humberto pushed the pedal to the metal, the ancient shelter van made its way through the South Bronx before rolling down FDR Drive along the East Side of Manhattan. Even though Manhattan was only a few miles from the Bronx, Tyrell could count the number of times he had been there on one hand. Everything was shinier and taller in Manhattan. The highway followed the curve of the East River, which sparkled with late-afternoon sunlight.

In the front passenger seat, Marcus had his cell phone pressed to his ear, talking to a police officer. Mrs. Yang looked as if she could throw up at any second, which was exactly how Tyrell was feeling.

Maybe they had something in common after all.

Humberto pulled off the highway and navigated the streets of downtown until signs changed from English to Chinese. Vendors were lined up along the streets, selling odd-shaped vegetables and spiky fruits he had never seen before while people pushed their way along the crowded, narrow sidewalks. There were lots of handbags and touristy New York City T-shirts for sale. Even though he was half Chinese, Tyrell had never been to Chinatown, and his dad had never talked about his family or their culture. For the first time, Tyrell felt interested in learning more.

Humberto pulled over to the side of the street right next to the school, wedging the van into a spot in front of a No Parking sign. Marcus, Tyrell, and Mrs. Yang jumped out and June ran toward them.

"I've checked all the classrooms," she said, her face flushed. "She asked to go to the bathroom ten minutes before dismissal and never came back." Then she looked at her mom and quickly spoke in Chinese.

"Marcus!" a voice called out. They all swiveled to find Ms. G running toward him.

Tyrell sprinted toward her and flew into her waiting arms.

"Hey, Tyrell," she said, hugging him tight. "I've missed you."

"How did you know we were here?" he asked.

"Marcus texted me. I don't live far, so I came by to see if I could help."

Marcus finished talking to a policeman, then looked at

June. "You know her best. Think about where she might have gone."

June furrowed her brow. "She might have gone to our old apartment building."

"Okay, you go there." Marcus pulled a disposable cell phone out of his bag. "Take this. It's the shelter's emergency phone. My number is already in the contacts. Humberto will go with you."

Mrs. Yang said something in Chinese, then joined June. They headed off toward their old home.

Tyrell felt useless standing there with nothing to do. While Marcus updated Ms. G on what he knew, Tyrell sat on the edge of a concrete planter filled with rocky soil, scanning the sidewalks for Maybelle. Why would she leave school? Where would she go?

Then Tyrell stood up and grabbed Humberto's phone from the clip on his belt. He knew exactly where Maybelle was.

"Hey, give that back!" Humberto said.

But Tyrell was already opening the internet browser and typing in *animal rescues Chinatown NYC*. The answer popped up within seconds: Mott Street Animal Shelter.

"I know where she is," Tyrell said, showing them the phone.

Marcus nodded. "Take Humberto with you. We'll stay here in case Maybelle comes back to the school."

Tyrell followed the instructions on Humberto's phone, running as fast as he could to Mott Street. The sidewalks were clogged with tourists haggling over the price of souvenirs. He raced by a store with a completely open front with bins of glassy-eyed dead fish on ice, then a meat store with animal carcasses displayed in the windows. No wonder Maybelle was a vegetarian.

Tyrell made it to Mott Street Animal Shelter before Humberto, who was a block behind him, huffing and puffing. He burst into the lobby and there was Maybelle, surrounded by people wearing Mott Street Animal Shelter T-shirts, her face wet with tears as she sobbed, her skinny arms around a dog that Tyrell assumed was Nana.

Tyrell dropped to the floor next to her, and Maybelle pulled him into a three-way hug with Nana.

"Maybelle, you scared us so much," Tyrell said.

"I'm sorry," she said, her voice muffled by Nana's fur coat. "I just wanted to see her again."

He watched Nana lick Maybelle's tears as Humberto grabbed his phone and called Marcus and June.

A few minutes later, June and her mom flew into the room.

"I can't believe you did this," June said, looking as if she might cry. "Don't ever scare us again."

Then Mrs. Yang grabbed both of her daughters and pulled

them so close that Maybelle and June looked like they might suffocate. She said something in Chinese, and June burst into tears. And suddenly, June, Maybelle, and their mom looked like a unit. A family.

That familiar loneliness—the voice that whispered that no one was in his corner—sank over Tyrell as he watched them.

FIFTY-SEVEN

June

NGÓH JAN HÁIH HÓU DEUIM̀HJYUH, MOM HAD said to them. *I am so sorry.*

Ngóh hóu sek néih, Mom told them. *I love you very much.*

June had been waiting to hear those words for so long. A flood of memories engulfed her.

Of coming to the Mott Street Animal Shelter each day after school with Maybelle.

Of walking Chinatown's narrow streets filled with vendors and vegetable stands and fish laid out on ice.

Of walking with her dad on Saturday morning, picking up groceries for the week and coming home with fruits in pink plastic grocery bags and fresh pastries still warm from the oven.

Of going to the playground with her mother and May-belle and watching the seniors from the neighborhood lined up on the concrete doing morning tai chi in a beautiful display of synchronized movement and strength.

But then, when she looked up and saw Tyrell and Marcus and Ms. G, June realized that even though she had spent her whole life in Chinatown, Huey House and the people who lived and worked there were starting to feel like home too.

Marcus's teasing and joking.

Mamo's cooking, which had expanded to include more vegetarian options, which were actually quite good.

Domenika and Bartók and her cluttered home.

And, of course, Tyrell, who had rapidly become one of the best friends June had ever had.

Home was a funny thing. You thought it meant one thing, only to discover that it meant something else entirely.

FIFTY-EIGHT

Tyrell

TYRELL TRIED NOT TO FEEL BAD ABOUT sitting by himself in the middle row of the van on the way back from Chinatown. Marcus took the front seat and made phone calls, letting everyone know that Maybelle was safe. Humberto was in the driver's seat, humming along to his mariachi music.

June, Maybelle, and Mrs. Yang were all crammed in the back row, murmuring in voices so quiet that Tyrell couldn't hear even when he leaned his head way back, pretending to stretch. The Yangs were in their own family bubble now, and he knew it wouldn't be long until they too left Huey House.

"You're a hero," Marcus said over his shoulder, interrupting Tyrell's thoughts.

Tyrell turned to look out the window. The East River was frothy and full of waves. A big ship had just swept through, disrupting the waters.

"I heard from Jeremiah last week," Marcus said.

Tyrell didn't reply. Waves crashed against the rocks, right next to the highway.

"He asked about you."

"I'm fine."

"Are you?"

Tyrell didn't respond, but he didn't look away from the river either. He blinked back tears. Real men didn't cry.

Everyone knew that.

9

When the van reached Huey House, Tyrell's eyes were heavy and itchy. Luckily, everyone was so happy to see Maybelle safe and sound that no one paid any attention to him. Stephanie passed him a letter as he signed in, and Tyrell shoved it into his pocket. It was probably one of those welfare letters for Mom, or another letter from his dad that he wouldn't open.

Tyrell made his way down the hallway, then out the back door. The backyard had been cleaned up, the four trailers now taking up all the space. Thinking back to the last time he'd been there, when he overheard the HQ people talking, he realized that nothing he'd done to fight the new housing policy had worked. Not the mice, not the letters, and not the phone calls.

He felt stupid for having thought he could make a difference.

It was weird being out here now that families were living in the trailers, so he went back inside and downstairs to the chapel. It was quiet there, so different from the days when he and Jeremiah would think up pranks or dream about their futures. When he sat on a pew, he felt the letter crease awkwardly in his front pocket.

He pulled it out. There was no return address; his name was the only writing on the envelope. It was probably from Marcus, who sometimes liked to leave notes about how he was so proud of him.

The letter inside wasn't from Marcus. The words were penned in a stiff, unfamiliar handwriting.

Dear Tyrell,

My name is Juan Ortiz. I recognized you the other day when you walked by my store, but you ran away before I could talk to you. I followed you here because I wanted to share something, but it did not seem like the right moment. I am writing this letter in hopes that it will bring you peace.

My brother was Bolívar Ortiz, and I now take care of his son, Nicolas.

Nicolas looks like his father, and you look like yours. Like Nicolas, you are growing into your own person. Our past does not have to dictate our future. You are your own man with your own path and the power to determine who you want to be.

I pray every day for Nicolas to grow into a strong, brave, and noble man, and I pray the same for you. I want to let you know that we extend love and forgiveness to you and your family. May God bless you.

Sincerely,

Juan Ortiz

Tyrell read the letter slowly once, then twice, then three times. The words stood clear on the white paper and went straight into his heart. He folded the letter and slid it back into the envelope, pulled his instrument case from under the pew, and took his violin out. He ran his fingers over the smooth wood, put the violin on his shoulder, and began to play.

It was as if his fingers were moving on their own, making music that spoke the deepest fears and desires of his soul, things he had never been able to say out loud. He let his bow arm get heavy on the strings, rich notes pouring from the instrument. The music spoke of the words from Juan Ortiz, a man he had never talked to but who was linked to him forever through the worst tragedy. A man who could extend the forgiveness Tyrell desperately needed.

Tyrell didn't notice the door to the chapel opening, not until his violin was joined by the chocolate tones of June's viola. Together, the notes tangled and separated and weaved above and beneath each other. June seemed to anticipate what Tyrell would do, her viola finding perfect harmony with his violin. At the end, the notes shimmered in the air, then faded into the chapel.

Tyrell placed his violin on the pew behind him and pulled out the letter from Juan Ortiz. He handed it to June. "My dad killed a man," he told her. "This letter is from his brother."

She took it, read it, and handed it back. Then she wrapped her arms around him in a hug and said, "Tyrell, I didn't know. I'm so sorry."

Tears rolled down Tyrell's face and his body shook from the struggle of having to keep it all together for so many years.

"We're going to be okay," June said, weeping with him.

And at that moment, in that quiet chapel, Tyrell believed her.

WEDNESDAY, OCTOBER 24

Days at Huey House
Tyrell: 1,299; June: 25

FIFTY-NINE
June

WHEN JUNE WOKE UP ON WEDNESDAY, SHE was surprised to find her mom helping Maybelle get dressed. It had been months since June remembered her doing that. Maybelle was sleepy and limp while Mom pulled a sweater over her tired body.

"Thanks, Mom," June said. She changed, then brushed her teeth. Before June could grab their backpacks and head out the door to the bus, Mom stopped her and spoke to her in Chinese.

"I'm trying to get better," she said. "Ms. G has been helping me."

June stopped. "Ms. G?"

"She got me a counselor who speaks Cantonese," Mom said.

"Wow," June said.

"I see her twice a week and we talk. I'm taking medicine."

"Wow," June said again.

"She's helping a lot," Mom said.

"I'm glad," June told her, and she meant it.

"I'm sorry about the last year," Mom continued. "I was so sad. I should have taken care of you and Maybelle. I hope you will forgive me."

June didn't know what to say to that, but hope bloomed in her chest.

Maybe their luck was finally turning around.

SIXTY
Tyrell

TYRELL USED TO LOOK FORWARD TO WEDNESDAYS, when he had his family counselor meetings with Ms. G, and fresh-baked cookies were always waiting for him. Now he dreaded those meetings. It wasn't just that he had to go to Mr. Fernsby's office with his mom, sit on cold metal folding chairs, and fill out forms. It wasn't even that Mr. Fernsby was super bland and boring.

The worst part about Wednesdays was that Mr. Fernsby had moved into Ms. G's office, and being in there made Tyrell miss her a million times more. Her office had been transformed. No more purple couch, no more cookies, no more fried chicken or lasagna with way too much cheese baked into it.

Today, however, was much, much worse than any other Wednesday.

"So—*ahem*—I think you're—*heh*—ready to move," Mr. Fernsby said after a few minutes of sorting out his paperwork.

"Move!" Ma exclaimed.

"The—*heh*—city's shelter-to-home program is beginning, and we need to get more—*heh*—families into housing now. An apartment that accepts vouchers opened up in Jamaica. I think it will be a good fit for you."

"Jamaica!" Tyrell blurted out. "That's not even in this country!"

Mr. Fernsby paused from his paper shifting to look at Tyrell over his glasses. "Jamaica, Queens. A—*heh*—nice neighborhood."

"We've never lived in Queens," Ma said. "We've always lived in the Bronx."

"Jamaica is right by the airport," Mr. Fernsby continued.

"For all the air travel we do?" Tyrell asked. He had never even been on a plane.

"What about Tyrell's school?" Ma asked.

"He can transfer. I'll start filling out the paperwork."

"Don't you dare," Ma said, standing up. "I don't even have a job."

"Then you better get one," Mr. Fernsby said. "You've been

here for three and a half years. It's time to move on." He signed his name with a flourish on a piece of paper. "Your move date—*heh*—is next Tuesday."

9

Tyrell felt sick. There was no way he and Ma would be ready to leave in six days. He went down to dinner but couldn't eat a thing, and afterward he followed his mom, Abuela, Lulu, June, and a handful of other residents up to Ms. Vega's room. While Ms. Vega washed Ma's hair in the bathroom sink, people compared notes about what Mr. Fernsby had told them.

"I'm only a few months away from getting my license, but he wants to move me out now," Ms. Vega said as she washed Ma's hair.

"Well, I can't wait to move out of this dump," Ma said. "Imagine having a kitchen again!"

"Will there be food in it?" Tyrell muttered. Ma couldn't hear him over the sound of the faucet, but June, who was sitting next to him, could. June's and Tyrell's eyes met.

"You're going to have a kitchen?" Abuela asked.

"Jeremiah's apartment has a kitchen, a living room, *and* a dining area," Lulu said.

"How do you know?" Tyrell asked.

"Marcus told me," Lulu said.

"Jeremiah's mom went through a special program that Ms. G helped them get into," Abuela said. "It's nothing like this new program."

"So our new place won't even have a *kitchen?*" Tyrell asked.

"I don't think you should expect much," Abuela said. "Sarah moved out on Monday and said they put her in an old motel in Ozone Park, two miles away from the nearest subway station."

Tyrell watched as Lulu put on an apron and went through the motions of sweeping the floor, tidying the hair supplies, and disinfecting the combs and scissors. The swish of the broom against the ground, the slosh of the cleaning solution, and the gentle clicks of hair clips were all so familiar. They were part of the soundtrack to Tyrell's life, and his throat closed at the thought of never seeing Lulu or Ms. Vega again.

It seemed unbelievable that Huey House as he knew it was coming to an end.

THURSDAY, OCTOBER 25

Days at Huey House
Tyrell: 1,300; June: 26

SIXTY-ONE

June

JUNE KNEW IT WAS ONLY A MATTER of time before her family got their housing notice. Mr. Fernsby was building momentum, and it was all anyone could talk about in the cafeteria. Along with Lulu's and Tyrell's families, several others had gotten moving dates. June was sure more news would greet her when she got home, but at the moment she had other things to worry about. It was her first day of orchestra rehearsal. They were going to work on her viola concerto.

Because rehearsals were after school on Tuesdays and Thursdays, Marcus arranged for Humberto to drive down when school was done, pick up Maybelle, and bring her to visit Nana while June went to orchestra. After rehearsal, they would pick June up and head back to Huey House.

June was about to open the door of the orchestra practice room, also known as the cafeteria, when she noticed someone also reaching for the door handle. She looked up to find Henrietta Woo, the best violinist in the school, the person June had admired for so long and the reason she'd wanted to be in the orchestra in the first place.

"Hey," June said, glad to have the opportunity to introduce herself. "I'm June, and I just wanted to say that I'm so happy—"

"I know who you are," Henrietta said, her eyebrows drawn together.

June froze.

"You have the viola solo. I think it's ridiculous that we're doing a *viola* concerto. Vivaldi never, ever wrote a concerto for viola. This"—Henrietta held up a fistful of sheet music—"is transposed. It's not even really Vivaldi. His best concertos were for violin."

June didn't respond as Henrietta pushed past her into the cafeteria. Henrietta was right: the concertmaster was always the best violinist and usually got the solos, and the concerto they were playing had been transposed for viola. She wasn't sure what Ms. Tang, the conductor, was thinking, either.

Henrietta's words repeated themselves over and over in June's head as she made her way toward the creaky folding chairs. At least the viola section was a safe distance away from the first violins. Henrietta sat in the concertmaster seat and flicked her glossy hair over her shoulder while she unpacked her instrument.

June took out her own instrument and tuned, and Eugene —a cellist—sat in the chair next to her.

"Are you excited?" he asked as he rubbed rosin on his bow.

June shrugged and set her music on the stand in front of her, noticing that her hands were shaking. She glanced at Henrietta, who was talking with a few people in the first violin section. They were laughing and looking at June.

"I don't think Henrietta's very nice," Eugene observed. "Ignore them. You're going to rock the solo."

June swallowed.

"Hey, want to hang out after practice?" Eugene asked. "We haven't gotten bubble tea in forever."

"I . . . can't," June said, not looking at him. She knew he was worried about her, but it never seemed like the right time to tell him what had happened to her home and where she now lived.

When Ms. Tang entered the cafeteria, she yelled, "Musicians! Are you ready? The rhythm for the first page should be perfect, yes?" Everyone hurriedly shoved their instrument cases under their chairs, except for the cellists, who had piled their huge cases up against the cafeteria wall. Henrietta, as concertmaster, led the forty-person orchestra in tuning. Ms. Tang gestured for June to come to the conductor's podium, which was really a wooden apple crate turned upside down.

Ms. Tang paced in front of the orchestra. "Antonio Vivaldi was a master composer," she began. "But before you can play his music well, you must know his story. His first full-time job was as maestro di violino at the Pio Ospedale della Pietà. It sounds like a fancy concert hall or music school, but it wasn't. It was an orphanage. The children who lived there were abandoned or orphaned, or their families couldn't provide for them anymore."

June felt her palms starting to sweat, a sense of panic washing over her. Did Ms. Tang know where she lived? She glanced at Eugene, who was looking right at her. She looked away.

Standing between Ms. Tang and Henrietta in the solo position, June could feel the heat of Henrietta's glare. She squeezed the neck of the viola to prevent herself from anxiously picking at the strings.

"Vivaldi spent years working at the orphanage and composed most of his major pieces there," Ms. Tang continued. "He taught the girls how to play instruments, and the most talented joined the Ospedale's renowned orchestra and choir.

Imagine, girls with no home being given an amazing musical education, playing concertos written and taught by Vivaldi himself."

June let those words sink in. What a beautiful sound that must have been. Italian girls three hundred years ago, girls like her, playing the same pieces her own school orchestra was playing.

"I want you to think about those girls while you play this. Girls who had no families but who came together and made beautiful music. Because when you play together, you become your own family. You have to listen to and respond to each other. If you do that, the music will be powerful. Let your instruments talk."

While the orchestra members set up their instruments and shuffled sheet music, June thought about the music she played with Tyrell the night before, and how it *had* felt as if their instruments were talking to each other. It had felt as if an unbreakable bond was being forged between them.

Ms. Tang spent some time working with the various sections—first violins, second violins, violas, cellos, wind instruments—correcting them where the rhythm was complicated or where their intonation needed work. Meanwhile, June stood there, awkward, with nothing to do but listen and absorb the mood of the music.

Finally, after a half hour of working, Ms. Tang gestured for everyone to try the piece together. Then she raised her baton and took a breath, and all the stringed instruments moved as one to begin the second movement of Vivaldi's Concerto in A Minor. Instruments faded slightly as June began her solo, the sound of her viola filling the cafeteria, the other instruments taking turns joining and leaving the music, tangling with her melody. She tried to keep her bow and fingers light, skipping over the strings like Domenika had shown her. They were just learning the piece, so most of the sections didn't sound that great. But near the end of the page, there were a few phrases that connected so beautifully together that it left her breathless.

When they finished, June set her viola down.

Ms. Tang was the first one to break the silence. "Not bad," she said, a smile playing on her lips. "There was one moment in that piece where there was a pure connection, did you feel that?"

Some of the musicians nodded.

"*That* is what we are chasing, that place where the instruments are singing together and everyone is listening. Keep up the good work, June."

June felt her face warm with the praise.

Ms. Tang clapped her hands. "I need to grab something

from my office. Henrietta, please run through measures fifty-three to fifty-eight with everyone. The rhythm has to be perfect. I'll be back in five minutes."

Ms. Tang flew out the door.

"Great job, June!" Eugene called from the cello section.

"That was amazing!" called one of the second violins.

Then an icy voice split the room.

"Good for someone who doesn't even belong here," Henrietta said.

June froze.

"Shut up, Henrietta," she heard Eugene say.

Henrietta did not shut up. She stared at June. "I saw you get off the bus yesterday morning. The *homeless* bus. My mom always says there are too many homeless shelters and all the taxes we pay are so people like you can get free housing."

People like you.

That delicate connection June had felt with the orchestra only moments before frayed and tore. She swallowed, unable to utter a word, and then Ms. Tang stepped back into the cafeteria with a binder of sheet music.

"Let's run through measures fifty-three to fifty-eight in sections," Ms. Tang said. "I need to hear each section play in one voice. First violins, you start."

They practiced for another thirty minutes. Once rehearsal

was over, June slung the straps of her viola case over her shoulders and walked out of the cafeteria.

She counted the number of steps that took her out the door.

Thirteen.

SIXTY-TWO
Tyrell

TYRELL WAS WALKING PAST THE LOBBY, ON the way to the chapel to practice, when he heard Marcus's voice.

"Hey, phone call for you," Marcus said, sticking his head out of his office.

"For me?" he said, stopping in his tracks.

"It's June."

Tyrell took the phone from Marcus. "Is everything okay?" he said into the receiver.

"I need you to come down here right away," June said. Her voice sounded funny.

"Down where?"

"Down to my school."

"Why? What's going on?"

"Just come, please."

June gave him directions by subway, and Tyrell hung up.

"What's going on?" Marcus asked.

He knew Marcus wouldn't let him go downtown by himself, but June needed him. So he lied. "She wanted me to give Domenika a message."

Marcus looked as if he wanted to ask more questions, but then his phone rang. Tyrell darted out of the office while Marcus was distracted and ran upstairs for his jacket and the emergency MetroCard Ms. G had given to him last month. He went back to the lobby, signed out, and jogged down the street toward the subway. Even though he had rarely left the Bronx, June's directions were easy to follow. The subway near Huey House was an express, and it was a straight ride down to Chinatown—no transfers. He caught the train just as it entered the station, and it only took him forty minutes to get down there. It made him wonder why June and Maybelle didn't just take the subway to school instead of spending hours on the school bus.

He found June, Maybelle, and Humberto hanging out in front of the school. Tyrell jogged over.

Humberto looked at his watch. "I hope you can get this school project done quick, because we've got to head back to Huey House in thirty minutes or Marcus will kill me."

"No problem," June said. "We'll be right back."

SIXTY-THREE

June

AS THEY WALKED SOUTH, JUNE FELT TYRELL grab her arm.

"What is going on?" he asked. "Why does Humberto think we're doing a school project?"

"We're going to City Hall," June said. She stepped up her pace, and she could hear Maybelle race to catch up with her.

"What? Why?" Tyrell asked.

"Because we need to talk to the mayor! We can't sit around waiting for someone to notice us. We need to tell the mayor what this policy is doing! You don't want to move to the middle of nowhere in a few days, do you?"

"I'm going to tell the mayor that she's making a big mistake," Maybelle said, out of breath from running.

"June!" yelled a voice.

June turned and was shocked to see Eugene running toward them. She faced forward again and walked even faster. They needed to get down to City Hall, and she really didn't want to waste valuable time talking to Eugene about what had happened earlier during rehearsal.

"Where are you going?" he asked, jogging to keep pace with her. "Listen, if you're upset about Henrietta—"

"I'm not upset about Henrietta!" June lied.

"Who's Henrietta?" Tyrell asked from behind them.

"You're going too fast!" Maybelle said.

"I'm not upset about Henrietta," June repeated. "If you really want to know, we're going to City Hall to talk to the mayor. We wrote letters, we made phone calls, but nothing is working and we're running out of time. We need to see her!"

"By just walking up to her office?" Tyrell asked. "I don't know if that will work."

"We've got to do *something!*" June said as they entered a gated park. In front of them loomed City Hall, a white stone building with a curved cupola.

"Do something about *what?*" Eugene asked, touching June's shoulder. "I don't understand what's happening. Please tell me."

At hearing the concern in his voice, June finally stopped

and turned to face her friend. He looked so worried, it wasn't fair to keep evading him like she had been. She took a deep breath. "I didn't know how to talk to you about this. Henrietta was right. We got kicked out of our apartment last month. I live in a shelter in the Bronx now."

"That's where she met me," Tyrell added.

"And it's where we met Jeremiah and Ms. Gonzalez and Marcus," Maybelle added.

"Thank you for telling me," Eugene said. "I'm really, really sorry." He paused. "But what does City Hall have to do with it?"

After June quickly described the new policy, they made their way to the steps of City Hall and looked up. There were metal police barriers everywhere. They ascended the stairs, where a man in a New York Police Department uniform stood at the entrance.

"Where are you going?" the police officer asked.

"To see the mayor," June said.

"Nope," the police officer responded.

"What if we have an appointment?" June asked.

"Do you have an appointment?"

June couldn't lie to an officer of the law. "No."

"Then you can't come in," he said.

"It's really important," Maybelle said. "Life and death."

"Everyone thinks their issue is life and death," the police officer said. "Go to the city website and log your complaint there."

"We did," June told him. "No one responded."

"I'm sorry, I still can't let you in," he told them. "You have to go now."

Tyrell dug in his pockets. "What about some jelly beans?"

The police officer firmly shook his head.

Defeated, June, Tyrell, Eugene, and Maybelle went back down the stairs. June felt as if the weight she had been carrying for the past year had gotten even heavier. She had done all she could to help her family and friends, but her best wasn't enough. They would all be moved to terrible apartments far away from everything and everyone they loved, and she wasn't sure her family or any of the families at Huey House would ever recover.

As she approached the bottom of the steps, a few people wearing suits were gathered to the side.

"We can put the platform here," a man wearing a shiny blue tie said. "And the podium will go here."

"Sounds good," said the woman next to him, jotting notes down on her notepad. "The mayor will be ready to go at four o'clock tomorrow. A press release will go out first thing in the morning."

June's skin got a tingly feeling. "Excuse me," she said to the group. "What's happening tomorrow?"

The woman looked at them and smiled. "Were you the group who got the tour for the Government Ambassadors program?"

Tyrell joined her. "Yes," he lied.

"I love seeing young people interested in government," the woman said, beaming at them. "Tomorrow the mayor is making a big announcement on her new policy initiatives aimed at ending homelessness."

"Wow," Maybelle said. "Ending *all* homelessness?"

"Yes," the woman said. "It's quite an impressive set of policies."

"The mayor will be here tomorrow?" June asked.

"Yes, and you should come since you're interested in how government works!" the woman said. "It starts at four."

June looked right into the woman's eyes. "We'll be here."

SIXTY-FOUR

Tyrell

AS THEY RACED BACK TO THE VAN—a few minutes from being late—Tyrell considered what they needed to do to prepare for the next day.

"We need to tell *everyone* we know to go," Tyrell said as they jogged up the street. "The mayor needs to see that people don't want these new policies."

"Yes," June agreed.

"I'll spread the news too," Eugene said.

"I can make signs," Maybelle said.

They got to the van and said goodbye to Eugene. Humberto grumbled about the time all the way back to the Bronx.

As they went up the highway past the shining skyscrapers and gleaming bridges, Tyrell was suddenly struck with doubt.

Millions of people lived in New York City. Would anyone listen to a few kids? How could they possibly convince the mayor to listen to them?

When they got to Huey House, they found Marcus standing by the door, his big arms crossed over his chest. He did not look happy.

"See you later," Humberto said, pulling the van out into the street to park it behind Huey House.

"Where have you been?" Marcus asked them. "It's six o'clock."

"It was a civic engagement lesson," June told him. "For school."

Tyrell nodded. That wasn't technically a lie.

But Marcus wasn't convinced. He stood there in front of the door and didn't move. June finally cracked and told him everything.

"Let me get this straight," Marcus said. "You want to go to the press conference tomorrow and talk to the mayor."

"Yes," June said.

"And bring a whole lot of people with us," Tyrell said. "So she knows that people care about this issue."

"And we want to make signs," Maybelle added.

"Can you help us?" Tyrell asked.

Marcus looked to the sky, then looked back down at them and nodded. "I can help, but I'm just warning you that people might not show up. It's late to be organizing something like this. I don't want you to be disappointed."

"We need to at least try," Tyrell said. He wasn't at all sure either whether their plan would work, but he knew they would regret doing nothing.

At dinner, June and Tyrell circulated to all the tables, telling everyone about the event. Abuela, Lulu, and Ms. Vega said they would come, but most everyone else had to go to work or weren't sure if they could make it. After dinner, they made a graphic on Marcus's computer about the press conference and he sent it to his contact list of shelter providers. Tyrell, only because he was desperate, sent an email about the event to his teachers, including Ms. Gruber.

Finally, after Marcus had gone home and June went upstairs to put Maybelle to sleep, Tyrell went to the lobby to use the Huey House phone.

He picked up the receiver and dialed the number for Jeremiah that Marcus had given him. It rang ten times before he was disconnected.

FRIDAY, OCTOBER 26

Days at Huey House
Tyrell: 1,301; June: 27

SIXTY-FIVE

June

THE NEXT MORNING, JUNE WENT TO THE lobby with Maybelle to catch the bus.

"Remember what we rehearsed," June told her.

"I *know*," Maybelle said. "I've got it!"

Jill, Ms. MacMillan's assistant, was behind the bulletproof glass of the security desk that morning.

"Just who I wanted to see," she said when she spotted them. "I was cleaning up a desk drawer this morning and there were all these phone messages for you and Tyrell. They're from Jeremiah."

"He called us?" June asked.

Jill slipped the notes across the desk.

Maybelle coughed. "I don't feel so good. My body feels all hot."

Jill looked at her in concern. "Honey, maybe you should stay home from school."

"Good idea," June said, grabbing the notes in one hand and leading Maybelle out of the lobby.

"Great job," June whispered to Maybelle.

"I'm very good at pretending to be sick," Maybelle whispered back with pride.

June glanced at the notes as they went down the stairs. She couldn't *believe* that Stephanie hadn't given them the messages. They walked down the hallway and let themselves into the chapel, which was already brightly lit. Tyrell was sitting on a pew, rubbing his eyes.

"It's not right that you get up so early every day," he told them.

"Guess what Jill just gave me?" June said, and she dropped all the notes into his lap. "Look at all these phone messages from Jeremiah. Stephanie never gave them to us."

"What?" Tyrell said, blinking, looking at the dozens of notes scattered over his lap.

"We need to call him and tell him about the press conference!" June said.

"I tried calling him last night," Tyrell said. "No answer."

"You did?" June said, then, "We should try again."

Tyrell agreed, and they went back upstairs.

"I heard you were sick," Marcus said when he saw Maybelle. "You don't look sick to me."

Maybelle grinned. "I'm not sick! But we have so many posters to make that we're skipping school."

Once he got over the fact that they had lied about Maybelle being sick, Marcus let them hide out in his office to call Jeremiah. The phone rang and rang, then disconnected, just like the night before. After three more tries, they gave up on calling him and worked on the posters instead.

Thankfully, Ms. MacMillan was at the Department of Homeless Services offices that day for meetings leading up to the press conference. A couple of hours later, Abuela spotted them in Marcus's office and then went around to every room in the shelter sharing the news and convincing people to go down to City Hall that afternoon. A few people even stopped by to make signs of their own. At noon, they had a huge stack of posters and were anxious about what the afternoon would bring when Marcus showed up with sandwiches and sodas.

"I arranged for Humberto to drive you down to City Hall in a couple of hours. Anything else you need?"

The kids looked at each other.

"I'm so glad you asked," Tyrell said.

SIXTY-SIX

Tyrell

TYRELL, JUNE, MAYBELLE, AND MARCUS STOOD ON the sidewalk, staring at Marcus's black motorcycle.

"If I had a car, I'd totally take you," Marcus said. "What about the subway?"

Tyrell nodded. "We need to take the 5 express train to Manhattan, transfer to the 6 local at Fifty-Ninth Street, then get on the M at Fifty-First Street and take that to Woodhaven Boulevard. From there it's a half-mile walk to Jeremiah's apartment."

Marcus whistled. "That's gonna take some time."

"Can Humberto take us?" Tyrell asked.

Marcus shook his head. "Humberto is picking up a new family to fill an empty unit. He won't be back until two thirty."

At that moment, as if the universe was smiling down on them, Domenika emerged onto the sidewalk, dragged by a jubilant Bartók.

"Why aren't you in school?" Domenika groused, looking more like a college student who'd pulled an all-nighter than a professional musician. "I was sleeping, and Bartók must have heard your voices. He woke me up and dragged me out here."

"Sleeping!" said Maybelle in amazement as she wrapped her arms around Bartók. "It's nearly two o'clock!"

"Domenika!" June said. "*You* can help us!"

"Help you what?" she asked.

"*You* have a car and *we* need transportation."

"Oh no," she said. "I've got a concert tonight, and I need the rest of the afternoon to rehearse. I can't drive anyone anywhere."

"C'mon, Domenika," Tyrell said. "Is this concert more important than the fates of thousands of homeless kids?"

There was a pause, and Domenika heaved a sigh that could have been heard miles away. "Fine. I guess the prime minister of Canada, who told me that he has been looking forward to this concert for months, is more forgiving than most people."

Domenika led the way down the street and stopped at one of the smallest cars they had ever seen. It was silver and very compact.

"Why is it so tiny?" Maybelle asked.

"It's a city car," Domenika said defensively.

"Marcus sure as heck won't fit in there," Tyrell observed.

"I'll stay here and make sure people know how to get down to City Hall," Marcus said. "Domenika, can you give me your cell number so I know where these kids are? You're a safe driver, right?" He looked skeptically at her pajama bottoms, flip-flops, and torn T-shirt that said I'M A VIOLINIST—WHAT'S YOUR SUPERPOWER?

"Of course I'm a safe driver," she replied, offended.

June climbed into the front seat while Tyrell, Maybelle, and Bartók got into the back with dozens of empty orange-soda bottles that were scattered on the seat and the ground. Marcus gave Jeremiah's address to Domenika, and she plugged it into her phone.

"I'm getting you a canteen for Christmas," Maybelle announced from the back seat. "All these single-use plastic bottles are bad for the environment."

Domenika turned around and glared at her. "Do you want a ride or not?"

Maybelle pursed her lips and didn't respond, but she did whisper into Bartók's ear, "Canteens rule."

Domenika turned on the ignition and squealed out of her parking spot, nicking the bumper of the car parked in front of her. Tyrell looked out the window and caught a glimpse of

Marcus, his brow furrowed and arms crossed, as Domenika accelerated down the street.

"So," Domenika said to June. "How did rehearsal go yesterday?"

"It went really—" June began before yelling, "Watch out!"

"I saw him," Domenika said breezily as she swerved and barely missed a man crossing the street with an aluminum walker that had tennis balls attached to the feet.

"Uh, Domenika? Bartók is starting to gag," Maybelle said.

"Quick, read to him!" Domenika said, removing a valuable hand from the steering wheel and leaning over to the glove compartment to grab a book. She tossed it over her shoulder.

"Watch out for that bus!" June cried.

"I saw it! Geez, June. You're never allowed in my car again," Domenika said.

"Good!" cried June.

Tyrell glanced at the book cover. "Oh no. I am not reading *that* book."

"Quick, Tyrell," Domenika commanded. "Trust me, you do not want to be in this car if Bartók throws up."

"June, you do it," Tyrell said, throwing the book into her lap like a hot potato.

"Reading in the car makes me sick," she informed him, tossing it back to him.

"Seriously?" Tyrell asked, shielding the cover art of a women with a very red, very low-cut dress being held by a shirtless, muscled man from Maybelle's eyes.

"Quick, Tyrell! Bartók's going to throw up all over me!" Maybelle said in a panicky voice. Bartók's gagging intensified, and drool hung from his jowl.

Tyrell opened the book to the first chapter. " 'Hazel was engaged to Sir Anthony Meekle. It was an arranged marriage, put together by her father. If only the man she really loved, the Duke of Hertfordshire, were a more appropriate partner. But he did not even know Hazel existed. And he had a line of women out the door who wanted to be his wife.' "

"It's working!" Maybelle said. "Bartók stopped gagging! Keep reading!" She rubbed behind Bartók's ear. "What does 'appropriate partner' mean?"

"Domenika, I don't think this is suitable literature for six-year-olds," Tyrell said.

"Watch out for the tractor trailer!" June shrieked.

"Bartók is gagging again!" Maybelle yelled. "Tyrell, read!"

Tyrell began again. He read while Domenika wove through traffic as if she were a veteran taxi driver, and June gripped her seat belt and shouted when they got too close to hitting something or someone.

Meanwhile, Maybelle was engrossed in the story, and Tyrell hated to admit it, but he was getting into it as well.

They had gotten to the part where the duke runs into Hazel at some type of fancy dance where people were *waltzing*—go figure!—when the car screeched to a stop in front of an apartment building made of red brick. Neatly trimmed bushes lined the path to the entrance.

"We're here!" Domenika announced.

SIXTY-SEVEN

June

JUNE, TYRELL, AND MAYBELLE RAN TO THE apartment building, Bartók galloping beside them. After locating the silver call box, June buzzed Jeremiah's apartment number. They waited a few seconds, then buzzed again. Tyrell glanced at his watch.

"It's two fifty-one," Tyrell said. "The press conference starts at four."

"Maybe he isn't home from school yet," June said.

As Tyrell reached for the buzzer again, they heard a voice behind them.

"Tyrell?"

They turned. Jeremiah stood there, looking as if he were staring at ghosts. Then he stepped toward Tyrell, grabbed him in a hug, stepped back, and punched his shoulder. "How come you haven't called me back? I left fifty messages!"

"Ouch!" Tyrell said, rubbing his shoulder. "Stephanie didn't give them to us!"

Jeremiah looked at them in suspicion. "Really?"

"Really," June chimed in. "We only got them this morning."

"Woof!" Bartók added, corroborating their accounts.

And then everyone started to talk (and in Bartók's case, bark), so only a jumble of words could be heard. *City Hall* (Maybelle) and *We need your help* (June) and *I'm so sorry* (Tyrell). And then Tyrell pulled Jeremiah toward the tiny car where Domenika was not-so-patiently waiting.

"We're running out of time!" Tyrell said, yanking Jeremiah's arm. "We've got to get to City Hall."

As if she had heard him, Domenika put her hand to the car horn and pressed.

"Took you long enough!" she said when they reached the car.

Jeremiah squeezed into the back with Tyrell, Maybelle, and Bartók. Domenika squealed out into the street, executed an illegal U-turn, and headed back toward Queens Boulevard.

"I hope people show up," Tyrell said, looking worried.

June looked out the window. Even though she tried to take deep, calming breaths, her mind was filled with worries. What if no one was there? The mayor definitely wouldn't take them seriously if it seemed like no one cared. What would they do then?

Before anyone could say more, Bartók started gagging again, and Tyrell grabbed the novel he was sitting on and started reading out loud.

Jeremiah glanced at the cover. "Why are you reading a book with two nearly naked people on the cover?"

SIXTY-EIGHT
Tyrell

THERE WAS QUITE A BIT OF FRIDAY traffic, and four o'clock was inching up on them. While Tyrell read to the enraptured Bartók and Maybelle, June and Jeremiah kept an anxious eye on the clock. Domenika zipped along the matrix of highways, cutting in front of taxis and tractor trailers and airport shuttles, while June periodically shrieked or yelled, "We're going to die!"

After half an hour, Domenika pulled off the highway and they entered Chinatown. The narrow streets were lined with cars as far as Tyrell could see.

Domenika screeched to a stop. "Time to get out of here and kick some butt at City Hall."

"We're here?" Tyrell asked, not recognizing the area from the day before.

"No," Domenika said, "but close enough. There's a huge traffic jam in front of us. You have to run two blocks that way. I'll come as soon as I find a parking space."

They grabbed their stack of signs and scrambled out of the car while Domenika held Bartók's collar. When they closed the door, Bartók smashed his face against the window and they could hear him howling.

"What if no one's there?" Tyrell asked again, his stomach churning at the thought. Would the mayor listen to just a few kids?

"I see City Hall!" June said, pointing to a huge white building surrounded by trees and a black iron fence.

Tyrell broke into a run. Down the block he spotted people—lots of people! Many of them were wearing bright orange T-shirts. They couldn't be there for the press conference, could they?

As they got closer, Tyrell recognized lots of folks from Huey House. Lulu, Ms. Vega, Abuela, Marcus, Humberto, Mamo, and dozens more. Ms. G was there as well, talking to Marcus, along with Ms. Hunter and even a few of the Cressida girls still wearing their school uniforms.

Then he saw his principal and a whole bunch of teachers

and students from his school, including Ms. Gruber, his scary English teacher. She was carrying a sign that said SAFE SHELTER IS A HUMAN RIGHT. They were all wearing orange shirts. Preschoolers and kids he'd never seen before struggled to hold up big signs that shouted SAVE HUEY HOUSE and LOVE OUR NEIGHBORS. And then there were the reporters carrying microphones, and camerapeople with big equipment on their shoulders.

"June!"

Tyrell turned and saw Eugene running toward them.

"Eugene!" June cried. "Can you believe this crowd?"

"I sent an email to Ms. Tang and the orchestra last night, and I think people shared the event on social media!"

"What's up with the T-shirts?" Tyrell asked. All around him was a sea of orange.

"Some guy was passing them out. I think he was from a community advocacy group. Cool, right?" Eugene pulled his T-shirt straight so they could read the big white letters printed on it.

" 'Homeless, not invisible,' " Maybelle read out loud.

Tyrell looked around; the sea of people in orange T-shirts seemed to have grown by hundreds in just a few minutes.

"Come on, let's pass out the posters," Eugene said, grabbing one that said SAVE HUEY HOUSE.

They moved among the crowd, giving out the posters they had made earlier that day to anyone who wanted them.

The buzz of a loudspeaker and the sound of someone coughing into a microphone quieted the crowd.

The press conference was beginning.

SIXTY-NINE

June

JUNE, TYRELL, AND MAYBELLE PUSHED THEIR WAY through the crowd to the front while Eugene stayed back to pass out the rest of the signs. The microphone buzzed, and June watched as a mustached man wearing a black suit and a skinny blue tie tapped the microphone. The man, along with a bunch of other people wearing suits, stood on the steps right in front of City Hall.

"Thank you for coming," he bellowed, and the speakers screeched. He paused to let someone adjust the equipment, then said, "My name is Johnny Cleaver. I am the director of public relations in the office of the Deputy Mayor for Health and Human Services. We're so pleased to announce a new initiative today, a groundbreaking policy designed to get the homeless off the streets and into housing faster than ever."

"Save Huey House!" someone yelled from the crowd, and Johnny Cleaver looked up, startled at the interruption.

Johnny Cleaver coughed, then went on, "As I was saying, we're proud of the hard work of the Department of Homeless Services as they address the growing number of homeless families in the shelter system. As a result of their work, we're partnering with landlords all over the city to move families quickly into secure housing while they get on their feet."

"Bring back our job programs!" someone yelled from the crowd.

"We want *safe* housing!" someone else shouted, to cheers of agreement.

Johnny Cleaver looked back at his colleagues, then coughed again. "I wasn't expecting such a big group. It's, um, great to see you all here. So, er, we're excited to—"

"Don't give up on our kids!" someone yelled.

"Now, wait a second," Johnny Cleaver said. "This program is built to get homeless families into great housing—"

"We are not invisible!" someone chanted, and people joined in until hundreds of voices were yelling, "We are not invisible!" in unison.

June looked around at all the people who had shown up for them: Huey House and Ms. G and her classmates and members of her orchestra, all chanting, "We are not invisible." And before she knew it, she found herself striding up the steps toward the podium.

Johnny Cleaver put his hand over the microphone. "What are you doing?" he hissed as she approached, then looked behind him, where the mayor and other government staff were standing.

"Get her out of here," Johnny Cleaver said, only this time he forgot to cover the microphone. The crowd responded by booing him.

Lifting her chin, June leaned over and reached for the microphone. "Excuse me, can I just say something?"

Johnny Cleaver yanked the microphone back toward him. "Of course you can't say anything. This is a government press conference—"

But Johnny Cleaver didn't get to finish.

Because now Tyrell and Jeremiah had joined June at the podium.

"Let her speak," Tyrell said.

"Let her speak!" the crowd chanted.

"Let her speak," a voice said from behind June, and she looked over her shoulder and saw someone looking directly at her.

That voice belonged to the mayor of New York City.

SEVENTY

Tyrell

JUNE SEEMED AWESTRUCK AT THE SIGHT OF the mayor, suddenly speechless. So Tyrell pulled the microphone toward him.

"We live at Huey House, a family homeless shelter in the Bronx," he said. "I've been there for over three years, and the place has saved my life. I learned how to read there. I'm learning how to play the violin. We don't want to get moved out into horrible housing in the middle of nowhere just because the government wants people to see lower homeless numbers."

"Now, wait just a second—" Johnny Cleaver said.

Then, to Tyrell's surprise, Jeremiah leaned forward and took the microphone. "I lived in Huey House for over three years too. My mom took a job training program there, and

Ms. G—she's the family services director—changed everything for us. She helped my mom get a steady job with benefits, and we just moved into a safe apartment in a nice neighborhood. I owe Huey House everything."

The crowd cheered.

"Okay, you've had your say—" Johnny Cleaver interrupted.

"Wait," the mayor said to Johnny Cleaver. Then she turned to June, Tyrell, and Jeremiah. "Go on. Please."

Tyrell looked at June. It was time for her to speak.

SEVENTY-ONE

June

TYRELL STEPPED ASIDE AND NUDGED JUNE TOWARD the microphone.

June cleared her throat. "Oh, uh. I just wanted to say—"

"Pull the microphone closer," the mayor coached her.

June adjusted the microphone and looked out into the crowd. In front of her were hundreds of people in orange T-shirts. Everyone was quiet and watching, waiting.

"Superhero pose," Tyrell whispered to her.

June stood up straighter. "Hi, I'm June Yang," she said with only the slightest wobble in her voice.

"Yay, June!" yelled Eugene from somewhere in the middle of the crowd.

She took a deep breath. "I came to Huey House a month

ago. After my dad was killed in a car accident, my mom had a hard time and stopped showing up for work. Our family ran out of money. When I first got to Huey House, I hated it. I just wanted to go home. But then I met friends, and we had a really good counselor named Ms. Gonzalez who got my mom the help she needed. I met an awesome viola teacher, and I guess what I'm trying to say is that the shelter has become a place where my family can . . . become whole again. We're here because we want the same things everyone else wants: safe housing and good schools. I think all kids deserve that."

The crowd cheered.

"I don't expect to live at Huey House forever," June continued when it was quiet again, "but it's been a place to get strong and get the help we need. Please don't force us out just to make your policies look good."

City Hall Park erupted in applause.

The next thing she knew, the mayor was shaking her hand. Then Johnny Cleaver shook her hand too, making sure he was facing the news crews. When the applause quieted down, Johnny Cleaver grabbed a microphone.

"What an amazing group of kids!" he boomed. "Thank you all for coming, and we look forward to our continued partnership as we fight homelessness in New York City! Have a great weekend!" he said, and switched off the microphone.

The crowd booed. "What about the policy?" someone yelled.

But then the mayor walked to the podium. She turned the microphone back on. "As the mayor, I don't always get to hear the voices of the people I serve. And sometimes, when we're trying to fix a problem, we dive too quickly into the easiest solution or whatever looks good on paper. I'd like to propose additional focus groups and an extensive review of the state of homelessness in our city before proceeding with any policy change."

A reporter ran up the stairs and pointed a microphone at the mayor. "Does this mean shelters will not be receiving cash incentives for moving families out within ninety days?"

"That is correct. I hope everyone hears this: I promise I will put my attention on this issue immediately." The mayor looked at June, Tyrell, and Jeremiah. "I promise to listen."

There was loud cheering from the crowd, sign waving from the protestors, and whistles from the orchestra members, and June felt hope blossom. Had they really saved Huey House? As the mayor closed the press conference, June stepped down from the podium and went to rejoin the Huey House group.

"Jèhjè," said a voice.

June turned, surprised to see her mom. "I didn't know you were here."

"Ngóh hóu hoi sum lei jo dut ho," Mom said, smiling. *I am happy that you are my daughter.*

June's spirit swelled with gratitude. "Thanks, Mom."

"Baba hóu hoi sum lei jo dut ho." *Your dad was so happy that you were his daughter.*

"Thank you," June said, tears collecting in her eyes as she preserved her mother's sentiments in her memory, the words a most perfect and precious gift.

Then, with a sense of certainty that her dad was indeed watching them from wherever he had gone, she glanced at her watch.

It was 4:44 p.m.

SEVENTY-TWO
Tyrell

TYRELL WATCHED JUNE AND HER MOM. HE waited for that panicked feeling—the one that told him he was alone in the world—to take over his thoughts.

This time, it didn't.

As the press conference finished and the crowd began to disperse, Tyrell wondered what the future held for him. He didn't know when he would move out of Huey House or what his next home would look like or whether he would one day play at Carnegie Hall like he dreamed. He guessed he just wouldn't know any of it until the days were delivered to him.

Lost in his thoughts, he found himself looking at Marcus, Ms. G, Lulu, Ms. Vega, Abuela, Mamo, Maybelle, Mrs. Yang, Domenika, June, and Jeremiah. The Huey House group had migrated to the steps of City Hall, where they sat talking and laughing as the sun cast a golden glow around them.

Marcus beckoned him to join them, and Tyrell walked over and took a seat between June and Jeremiah. A breeze whispered through the air and rippled the leaves of the trees arched above them, and at that moment it was as if the three friends shared one beating heart, the road before them belonging only to them — and filled with possibility.

MUSIC IN A DUET FOR HOME

Chapter Twenty-Six

Viola Concerto in G Major, first movement,
by Georg Philipp Telemann

Chapter Twenty-Seven

Lullaby by Johannes Brahms

Chapter Thirty-Nine

"Rêve d'enfant" by Eugene Ysaÿe
"Berceuse" by Amy Beach

Chapter Fifty-Four

Viola Concerto in G Major, fourth movement,
by Georg Phillip Telemann
Allegro by Shinchi Suzuki

Chapter Sixty-One

Concerto in A Minor, second movement,
by Antonio Vivaldi

AUTHOR'S NOTE

If you take the 2 or the 5 subway train into the South Bronx, get off at the Prospect Avenue stop, and head south, past the store selling spare parts for vacuum cleaners and sewing machines, you will eventually run into a plain brick building painted white and flanked by attached brownstones. The building used to be a hospital, but it isn't anymore.

To get in you need to be buzzed through two locked doors, show ID to security guards, be checked against the access list, then sign in on a battered clipboard. After that, you head out of the lobby, swing a right down a corridor with walls painted a vivid shade of green, and open a door at the end of the hallway that leads to a very narrow set of stairs into one of the brownstones. Once you're in the brownstone, big windows let in warm sunshine. Posters and artwork are taped to the brick walls. A trio of outdated computers is locked to a hexagonal table with thick cables. Go one floor up and you are greeted with a miraculous sight.

It is a library. A library so small it could easily fit inside a studio apartment in Midtown Manhattan. Wooden bookcases line the walls. Every shelf is heavy with children's books. You could say that the brownstone library is private — exclusive, even — because it is. Only kids who live in the attached building are allowed inside, because the building is a family shelter. The kids who have access to the brownstone library are homeless.

When I was twenty-one and right out of college, my first full-time job was at New York City's largest provider of transitional housing for homeless people. The organization's network of five family homeless shelters served nearly six hundred families every day. I worked there for four years as the assistant to the executive director, serving as a "multi-tool" of sorts. I was involved in everything from personnel to grant writing to program development to fundraising to research. In my last year working there, I taught literacy at the Bronx shelter's after-school program one afternoon a week, sitting in a child-sized wooden chair reading to kids and listening as they read to me.

One day, Steve, a second grader, swaggered into the library and slouched into the seat across from me. Steve didn't love to read. He struggled to sound out words, and often he was so focused on getting the words right that he reached the end of the page and had no idea what the story was about. To encourage him, I bribed him. "Every time I visit you," I told him, "we need to read two books. One book I choose; one book you choose. If you read to me every Tuesday afternoon, I'll take you to a Yankees game in May."

Steve didn't agree to this arrangement immediately. He tried to bargain it down to one book, but I was firm. He loved baseball, so he finally agreed when he realized I wasn't budging. We read lots of books together that school year.

After I met with Steve for three months, his reading skills improved. It was around then that he read *The Giving Tree* by Shel Silverstein for the first time. The book was my choice, not his; he preferred sports books or books with only a few words per page. At the end of the book, Steve slammed the cover closed and glared at me.

"This story's messed up. If I were the tree, I'd be like, forget you, boy. And you know what? I'm going to call him old man! He looks like an old man!"

Steve, who had endless patience with his younger twin brothers and charm enough to make even the crusty security guard stationed at the front desk smile, was close to tears.

"The tree gave everything," he told me, infuriated. "The tree gave up his whole life, and now he's just a stump. I'll *never* treat anybody like that. *Never.*"

The Giving Tree, seen through Steve's eyes, made me mad too. I thought about all the ways adults had let Steve down, all the disappointments he had experienced and all the broken promises he had listened to. When I got home that night, I threw my copy of the book in the trash.

By the end of May, Steve had earned those Yankees tickets. I still remember him looking out onto the baseball field for the first time from our nosebleed seats. "It's like a dream," he told me, his eyes never straying from the green.

Steve, his mom, and his younger brothers moved out of the shelter not long after that Yankees game. As it often does in the shelter system, the move happened fast. I didn't get to say goodbye to him. I didn't get to give him the stack of books I wanted him to take to his new home.

During my time working at the shelter, a new program called Housing Stability Plus (HSP) was rolled out by New York City's Department of Homeless Services. It was meant to respond to the dwindling supply of Section 8 housing vouchers, federal subsidies available to very low-income families that allowed them to find decent, safe, and sanitary housing in the private market. HSP, however, moved thousands of families into buildings with documented hazards such as lead paint, vermin, and lack of hot water and heat. The program was widely criticized and phased out three years after implementation.

In 2015, my husband and I took our two daughters to their first Yankees game. Coincidentally, we had received free tickets from our local library because our oldest daughter had read so many books during the summer reading challenge. Sitting there in the stands, I thought about Steve. He must have been eighteen by then, a young man looking out at the giant world. I wondered where he was. Did he do well in school? Was he going to college? What was his favorite book? Did he find a good library to spend time in? Did he still love the Yankees?

A few days ago, I reread *The Giving Tree*.

Once there was a tree, and she loved a little boy. And every day the boy would come and he would gather her leaves and make them into crowns and play king of the forest.

I will never forget those years I worked in the New York City shelter system and the year I spent teaching kids how to read. It was back then that the seeds of a book about the brave and resilient kids living in a New York City shelter began to germinate.

Twenty years later, here it is.

Karina Yan Glaser
2021

AUTHOR'S NOTE ABOUT THE CANTONESE IN THE BOOK

Cantonese, predominantly spoken in Hong Kong, Taiwan, and the Guangdong Province in mainland China, has a diversity of Cantonese romanization systems. However, there is not a widely held romanization standard like *pinyin* for Mandarin Chinese. I grew up with my parents speaking Cantonese to each other and their family, but like many new immigrants, they never officially taught my brother or me their native language.

The Cantonese in this book was written with the help of my cousin Josephine Kwok, who grew up speaking only Cantonese with her parents. She, along with a few other Cantonese-speaking friends and family, helped me translate the few phrases I needed for June's mom, which I also cross-checked with a handful of different Cantonese-language websites. I used commonly used, but not official, phonetic spellings and accents for the book and decided not to write out corresponding tone numbers to preserve the flow of the words on the page.

ALSO BY NEW YORK TIMES BESTSELLING AUTHOR KARINA YAN GLASER